Tarjei

Tarjei Vesaas was born on a farm in the small village of Vinje in Telemark, an isolated mountainous district of southern Norway, in 1897 and, having little taste for travel and an abiding love of his native countryside, died there in 1970 aged seventy-two. A modernist who wrote, against literary convention, in Nynorsk rather than the Danish-influenced literary language Bokmål, he is regarded as one of Norway's greatest twentieth-century writers. The author of more than twenty-five novels, five books of poetry, plus plays and short stories, he was three times a Nobel Prize candidate, although he never won the laureate. He did, however, receive Scandinavia's most important literary award, the Nordic Council Literature Prize. He first began writing in the 1920s, but he did not gain international recognition until the mid-1960s when Peter Owen first published his books in translation; since then they have appeared in many languages. The other work of fiction which, together with this novel, is generally regarded as his best is *The Ice Palace*, which Doris Lessing described as a 'truly beautiful book . . . poetic, delicate, unique, unforgettable, extraordinary'. At the time of his death he was considered Scandinavia's leading writer, and to this day coachloads of his fans go on pilgrimage to his farmhouse home.

Also published by Peter Owen
The Birds
The Boat in the Evening
The Bridges
The Ice Palace
Spring Night

TARJEI VESAAS

THE SEED

Translated from the Norwegian by Kenneth G. Chapman

PETER OWEN
London and Chicago

PETER OWEN PUBLISHERS
www.peterowen.com

Peter Owen books are distributed in the USA and Canada by
Independent Publishers Group/Trafalger Square
814 North Franklin Street, Chicago IL, 60610, USA

Translated from the Norwegian *Kimen*

First British Commonwealth edition 1966
This Peter Owen Modern Classic edition 2007
Reprinted 2022

ISBN 978-0-7206-1638-5

A catalogue record for this book is available from
the British Library

Printed and bound in Great Britain by
CPI Group (UK) Ltd, Croydon, CR0 4YY

Part 1: The Pit

1

THE TWO SOWS LAY large and heavy in their pens. Grey with caked mud. The pens were separated by a strong fence and were next to the barn. From these pens out in the open a narrow, dirtied door led into the pig pens inside.

The sun baked down and the sows grunted softly as they lay stretched out on the torn-up earth. Their grunting was a sound that seemed to bear witness to peacefulness, and to loneliness. But they were hardly lonely, the sound was deceptive.

They were mothers.

Each of them had a dozen or so of tiny young to take care of – they lay in a shining row beside the prostrate sow, lay there squealing and grunting and sucking. They had an agreement among themselves about the teats, and each had his own, but there still arose disputes, so that now and then small waves of discord swelled up. The sow paid no attention to this, and the waves soon subsided into satisfied grunts and snuffing while twelve small pairs of buttocks wriggled in sheer joy at being alive. In among these good sounds came occasional short, piercing, angry squeals when the milk failed to run quickly enough down the many throats. They toppled over on their smooth baby sides, and dozed. Now and then they peered up with their pale blue innocent piglet eyes.

It was like this on both sides of the fence. Tranquility, occasionally interrupted by short-lived dissonance. A strong, sour odor rose from it all, but those living in it never noticed it.

But still, there was something threatening latent in all this sleepy calm. It was not entirely convincing. Long naked tusks protruded all too plainly from ugly jaws, vicious teeth rooted in flesh – beneath the pitted, narrowed, overhanging brows.

But the baby pigs were pink and friendly, they shone with plumpness and an infant charm.

Suddenly the spell was broken: a sound came from the other side of the heavy board fence, from beyond the sow-pens. It was a strangely unaccountable sound, and it died away into itself. Stifled, for unknown reasons.

The sow lifted her head slightly, so that her lip fell down over her ugly tusks. She listened, undoubtedly expecting that there was more to come from the other side of the fence. But there was not, and she lay down again.

The baby pigs had sensed it only as an unconscious tensing. The milk flowed all too smoothly down their throats and into their stomachs. They concentrated on that. They were dry and comfortable in the sun, covered with silvery fuzz – and each had a teat all to himself. Just as it should be. The threatening sound did not come through to them.

The sow heard it. But she lay down again, and only showed her ugly tusks. She had heard her mate lift his voice. It appeared to be no friendly thought she sent him.

The boar lay beyond the fence, in an extra-strongly built pen. Lay there completely alone. Stretched out, lean and long and ugly. He was shut up in the hopeless wasteland he had made for himself. He had laid waste his yard so that not a blade of grass was left. Only mud and fruitless ground and dirty grey pebbles.

He was exceptionally unattractive with his lank body and wild bristles and the ravaged lines of his face. He was old and had had infinitely many children. He never saw them, only heard their clamor in the surrounding pens – the short time they lived there. They left as soon as they were a few weeks old. The boar stayed on, and grew uglier and uglier.

He pulled himself up on his front legs and sat there squinting. Life was boring. And it was much too hot.

His ears hung down over his jaws. He opened his wedge-shaped mouth in an empty, soundless yawn. From somewhere he heard the hum of young. Ten twelve fourteen at a time they came into the world, he knew nothing about it, but perhaps still knew about it. Never saw them. But there were surely many of them. He yawned, and forgot to shut his gaping mouth again.

Inside the summer-hot barn itself there was commotion and turmoil – in sharp contrast to outside. The youngest sow was having *her* swarm of young.

A girl sat there and saw that everything went as it should. But she sat staring and absent-minded.

The barn was full of buzzing flies. All the windows and doors were open. The strong sun intensified the odor from the pig pens. The flies buzzed dully, as if on the point of falling asleep in a dark corner.

The girl was young. She sat bent over on a stool. Leaned forward with her adolescent arms pressed against her breast. What was happening in front of her eyes was nothing new to her and it was going well, so it was something else that was causing her tenseness, her sadness. She thought: I'm not happy. Things should be different. How? I don't know, just somehow.

The pig pens were in one corner of a large red barn. On a farm on a small green and fertile island that lay in the middle of a bay that sheltered it from the storms farther out. There were many farms on the island. Between leafy groves and small cliffs. The earth was well cultivated and bore richly. Now it was late summer. Haying was over. Another crop was ripening.

It was a moment of rest on the island. The sort of half-holiday set by the crops and the weather. A time between harvests – that many people used to get a little extra work done, but that also many others just idled away, feeling they had earned it.

The mowed fields were green again, and the ripening grain shone. Soon there would be work enough. Maybe tomorrow. Some were far out at sea fishing. They would not return home that night, nor the next night. Most people on the island lived off the earth; it was willing and dependable.

But now all was calm, most like a sleepy Sunday. As on the farm with the dark red barn. No one was to be seen except the girl sitting in the barn.

The sows lay dozing. Rolled over so that the whole dozen of young found their teats. The baby pigs sighed in rosy contentment. The boar beyond the fence forgot to shut his jaws after the last yawn. The youngest sow gave birth. That was all.

2

JUST THEN A MOTOR was chugging out at sea, and an open boat neared the island. The boat docked at one of the small fishing piers and set a man ashore.

The man paid for the trip.

The men in the boat asked if they were to come and pick him up when he was finished there. He must have paid well.

'Finished here? What do you mean?' asked the man, a bit sharply. 'I'm not going back.'

'All right. Fine,' they replied quickly. But at the same time they noticed that he had no baggage. He became aware of this and added:

'Here's the receipt for my luggage back at the dock. You can go out and get it for me this afternoon. My name's on the slip: Andreas West.'

'We'll see to it,' they said and the boat chugged away from the island. They looked back at the man, but he was no longer watching them. He was busy looking over the island that lay before him.

He stood alone on the pier. Was not expected, and was not met by anyone. It appeared that he had never been there before, but that he had been longing to come: he looked around eagerly, thirsting for what he saw, for the growth and ripening on all sides that spiced the air already heavy with the smell of the sea.

A gentle voice seemed to say consolingly:

Andreas –

He listened to it. As if it were that he had hoped to hear. A veil passed over his timid eyes. He must have been seeing the sight he had been searching for. It was here! He was so sensitive and impressionable that he felt it with all his being. It was as if he wanted to express his gratitude for the sight. He breathed in the spiced air and then spoke, filled with love for what he saw spread out before him:

'The island is green – '

No one heard it. There was not a soul to be seen anywhere. The chugging of the motorboat was already fainter.

He was still standing on the pier. As if he were preparing himself for the joy it would be to step onto the island and gather up all that was beautiful and living there. He seemed to possess all the sensibilities needed to perceive and capture it.

Like a rejoicing:

A new place!

What I've been looking for so long is here – it must be.

See how it lies spread out –

Then he stepped onto the island. Onto the grass, and all that grew there. It gave softly under his feet, there was refreshment in each step, as if the soles of his feet were naked and burning and sore.

He felt somehow that he was welcome there. He was called by a soft voice that he felt rather than heard:

Andreas! Andreas!

Yes, he answered.

He heard the voice clearly inside him. It said his name as he stepped onto this rich island. He felt expected – because he thirsted for all that lived there and was growing and fertile. Therefore it was right for him to come and partake of these divine gifts.

Farms and homes lay here and there, with large trees in the yards, surrounded by meadows. The meadows were fringed by thick, leafy groves. Gardens, fruit trees everywhere.

Andreas West came to this island, on his frantic search for a place that could heal him. He was a young man, and healthy and strong and handsome, but inside he was seething and smoldering with restlessness, and the ugly memory of things that had happened to him. Things he wanted to forget, but could not. They had marked him, as had also all the restless wandering and seeking, and disappointment.

There had been many disappointments, one on top of the other. Everywhere he had come he had met things that hurt him and frightened him away again. The tension that shone in his eyes showed that he was about to give up. But then he would think he heard the voice again, calling to him from new, unknown places that perhaps could give him what he was seeking:

Andreas – come.

Yes, he answered, gripped, and turned immediately toward the secret calling and found no rest until he followed it.

What was he seeking?

Quiet. And peace. And all that was green. He had an uncontrollable desire to see things grow and unfold themselves according to their plans, to perfect themselves. To attain that which was perfection for each separate living thing.

It had come over him only recently. Since he had escaped with his life from the explosion at the factory. He had worked in the office. It was a large factory where dangerous raw materials were used. And one day it exploded. He could not free himself from the memory.

Wreckage. Fire. Death. Destruction. Even the earth had been singed and consumed.

Many of those who escaped with their lives had not had their nerves damaged, but he was not one of these. He had been injured without having received any external marks, had been filled with this restless searching for things he never found. For that peace that was for him, where everything could perfect itself. And with it was connected this simple thirst for green, fertile fields. To find those that were richest in fruit and ripening.

He wandered from place to place. Had not yet found what he was looking for. Nor had his restlessness decreased. He was ever as impressionable and sensitive to everything he met.

From place to place.

Now he had come to this island. And it was here, he believed as he stood there, and stepped ashore. He felt it with all his being: it must be here. It was here that he would finally be healed.

A whispering inside him told him that he had believed that many times before. You believe it every time you come to a new place. And every time you're wrong. You find nothing.

Yes, yes, but there'll be a time. And it must be here, since I feel the calling.

You'll never find it. It's nowhere.

But he was not listening to *that*. He thought: go away, it's not true. You're just a voice from that bad memory. That's how it was there. That's what we believed there. There was nothing else to believe then. But now it's different. Now we believe we can find a paradise.

Listen to the quiet call of welcome here:

Andreas –

I'll find peace here.

Peace? You're a bundle of nerves. Exhausted. Worn out.

That's exactly why it will be good to find peace.

He walked up the slight rise from the sea to the farms surrounded by groves. Spiced scents rose quietly and warmly from the earth.

He came to a bend in the road where two men sat quenching their thirst in the shade. They looked a little guilty at being seen taking time for such on a workday. It was easy to see that they were hard workers whose consciences bothered them as soon as they took a little rest. And now they had even been drinking beer.

One of them said:

'It's nothing to worry about.'

They saw it was a stranger who had come.

The other said:

'But we don't have to sit right in the middle of the road.'

They looked at the stranger without resentment, and asked right out where he was going.

'Nowhere in particular,' he answered, shy and helpless.

They laughed, and their happy, squinting eyes shone in their weather-beaten faces.

'Well, there's nowhere to go here, either,' they said. 'You're on a pretty small island. So you'll just have to stay here.'

'If you're thinking of going to church, it's on that island you see far off there,' they joked.

'And it's not Sunday, either,' they said.

'We have to use a boat to get to the minister,' they said.

'Sit down,' they said.

'No, thanks, I'm – '

He no longer wanted to see their beery faces. He began to walk away.

They were a little hurt.

'Our names are Hill and Dale,' they called after him. 'But we haven't asked for yours.'

They nodded good-naturedly at him and lifted their bottles to drink, but found that there was no beer left.

Andreas West just walked on. A large, dark red barn stood on top of a hill. He walked toward that farm. By chance. He had no errand anywhere. He just heard the call of the new friendliness he saw.

3

THE FARM WITH THE BIG RED BARN was called Lee. It was not only the farm with the largest barn, but also the largest orchard, on the island. The farmhouse, on the other hand, was old and small, but in good repair. There were two such small farmhouses. The owner, Karl Lee, had built the huge barn but then had come no farther. Had had to be contented with the other buildings as they were, even though they were too small. He had also planted the fruitful orchard, which gave him most of his living.

Mari Lee, his wife, and he himself and their two children worked the orchard. The rest of the farm, with fields and meadows and stock, was worked by others. So there were two families living at Lee. One in each house. They who worked the farm, and had done so for so long that they belonged there now, were a couple named Jens and Bergit, and it was their daughter Helga who was sitting watching the sow in the barn. They had only the one daughter, so they hired a man during the harvests.

Karl Lee had been born on the farm and had taken it over when his father died. Karl Lee was young then. But he had gone to school and studied other things first. Although his father had just barely been able to afford it, he had not objected, but worked hard and provided the money. It was what Karl wanted to do, so he had spent several years in town studying.

But that came to an end. His father died and Karl took over the farm – together with his mother. He really preferred living on the green island where he had been born after all.

He did three things at about the same time after he came home from school: he married a girl from the island, he planted a large meadow as orchard, and he built a barn that was much larger than seemed necessary at Lee. The largest building on the island.

He also intended to build a farmhouse in keeping with the barn. It was so easy to begin on things then, he was full of the exultation of feeling his own strength. His mother said that he would never be able to get all that building done, and that he was foolish. But she praised him for planting the large orchard. The other people on the island said that that's how it is when folks come straight from the books and try to work a farm.

The barn was raised and painted dark red, and shone against the bright green hillside. But it had cost so much that it put a stop to the other building plans. And children came as well. A son, Rolf, and a daughter, Inga. It was difficult enough keeping everything going, without building as well. So the barn stood there in all its glory, witnessing to a surge of strength that had duped Karl Lee when he was young. The barn at Lee. Big as the barn at Lee. – The people of the island had many such expressions. But they could all the same not help having respect for Karl Lee. There was something about him that demanded it.

His wife Mari and he had gotten along quite well together. They had quite simply had to, for the sake of the work, for the sake of the complex task they had taken upon themselves.

His mother had died before the orchard had reached maturity, but she did get to see the first fruits. She had said then that the orchard would make up for the barn.

When the orchard had matured, and really *bore*, tending it was so much work that they thought it best to separate it from the farm. They rented the farm out and kept the orchard for themselves. The orchard lay closest to their hearts because it was their own work. The farm had been inherited, they had done nothing to get it started.

The fruit from Lee became known at market, and they made out better than before. And Jens and Bergit, who worked the farm, made out well, too. Lee was a good farm and it had come to stand as a symbol of hard work and security.

Rolf was the older of the two Lee children and when he was seventeen years old he suddenly stood before his father and asked if he could study.

'Study ? What for ?'

'To show them!' answered Rolf stubbornly. 'I want to do as you did.'

He looked defiantly at his father.

Karl Lee was taken aback at this. He remembered all the endless shelves of books. He still had many books that he read when he had time for it. He had also passed his love of books on to his family; they all liked to read. Now Rolf stood there and defied something.

Karl asked:

'Show them? Who?'

'Oh –' was all Rolf answered, slowly.

'Aren't you well off enough here? And much better off than you'll be in a room in town. I know what *that* is. And it's not that you're afraid of working; I've seen that.'

Rolf had worked in the orchard so that it was a joy to see him.

'I think you'll get just as much out of life working here in the orchard, Rolf. And in some ways more than you could get other places.'

'I'll come back and work in the orchard.'

'You want to waste time like I did?'

'Yes, just like you did, that's what I want to do,' said Rolf emphatically. 'They can all just mind their own business!' he added when his father said nothing. 'Everyone who makes fun of us.'

Karl Lee was shocked at what he heard. That Rolf resented the old story about his unfinished studies. And now wanted to defy the neighbors by behaving in the same way.

'You don't have to get yourself all worked up, Rolf,' he said. 'We're not in disgrace.'

Rolf did not answer. His father continued:

'It's not necessary to make up for anything – thanks, but I've managed that myself.'

'You don't know,' said Rolf, 'how much it would mean to me to be able to do it. They've laughed at us.'

'We're not *so* thin-skinned,' answered his father. 'If *you* are, it'd be best to get over it.'

Rolf stood there and looked at him, afraid:

'Won't you let me?'

His father said nothing. Rolf *was* sensitive and touchy, he knew that. But he had never thought that that old nonsense about his studying and the barn had eaten at him. But he had no way of knowing what lay hidden in this withdrawn boy's thoughts. He had never been too close to Rolf. It was probably rare that a father and son were, they both had things for themselves and were reluctant to give themselves away. But he had gotten along well with Rolf and they had been friends. They had all been interested in the work in the orchard; been proud of it, and thankful for it. Rolf and Inga had worked there from the time they could first be of use. Inga was Rolf's closest companion. And the only one, too. He had never had much to do with the other boys on the island. Was it that crazy barn that was the cause of this isolation? It had not occurred to him before that Rolf was so sensitive to the criticism of the neighbors – especially since the farm had become something.

He himself, Karl Lee, had not the slightest feeling of being a failure. The orchard had brought him respect from all quarters.

But there stood Rolf. Despite everything. Wanted to study. The thought of losing his good help with the work even was not pleasant.

'Won't you let me?' Rolf asked again.

'I don't understand it.'

'But I told you I'd come back.'

'I'm afraid you won't,' his father said, 'once you've left – '

'I *want* to take over the orchard some day, but I've got to do this first.'

'Wasted!' said his father before he realized what he was saying.

Rolf answered quickly:

'Do *you* think it was wasted time to study?'

'No.'

No; each day he had been glad that he had been able to study. It had helped in ways he had never imagined it could.

'No, it wasn't,' he repeated, because a feeling of thankfulness rose up in him.

Rolf waited for an answer.

'We'll think about it; I'll give you an answer soon. Have you said anything to your mother about it ?'

'Not yet.'

'Then I'll talk to her first,' said Karl Lee.

He did. Told her what was gnawing at Rolf.

'Well, you know how Rolf is,' was all she said.

'How ? I know so little – '

'We know he's sensitive.'

'Is that why he's never had much to do with anyone ? Other than Inga.'

'I don't know; I suppose so. Oh, that silly barn of yours, Karl.'

'Do you hate it, too ?'

'Sometimes, maybe – '

'I wouldn't have it any other way,' he said.

'Not even when it harms your children ?'

'It doesn't; that's just Rolf's imagination.'

'They become so strange,' she said suddenly; 'neither of them tell me anything now that they've begun to be grown-up. Now they keep everything to themselves that doesn't concern the work or other daily things.'

'Yes, that's how it is, it seems.'

'I wouldn't have believed it,' she replied bitterly.

'And now Rolf will be leaving. For we'll have to let him.'

'Yes, but he'll come back,' she said, frightened.

They were working in the orchard. Rolf waited for an answer. They could see that Inga was also waiting for it. Rolf let Inga in on all his plans, they were sure of that. They saw it with envy.

'We'll have to manage it, then, Rolf, since you feel it's so important.'

'Thanks,' said Rolf.

Rolf was allowed to leave. Inga cried when he left. Rolf was home only during vacations and Karl Lee had to hire a man in his place.

Rolf was home in the middle of the summer, when the fruit was ripening in the orchard. He liked to work and was often out in the fields with Jens when there was nothing to do in the orchard. His parents only hoped that he would soon come home for good.

They also knew that he had been going with a girl from the island lately. Her name was Else. That was another tie to the island, they hoped.

Rolf was twenty now.

Inga was seventeen. It was not yet decided what she would do. But soon a decision would have to be made. It appeared that she wanted most of all to stay with the orchard.

She liked nothing better than searching for all sorts of plants in the fields and woods of the island. People met her at it every now and then – and liked meeting her. She had a couple of girl friends who were older than herself. Now that Rolf had left she was not as happy as before.

Karl Lee had asked Jens early that day if he wanted to go with him in the motorboat down the fjord to the small town there. They would be back shortly after dinner. He had a little errand there.

'No,' Jens had answered, 'the youngest sow is about to bear and it would be best for me to be home in case something happens.'

'Well, then I'll go alone,' said Karl Lee.

Jens was an ardent pig-raiser, so that one end of the barn at Lee was always full of the noise and tumult of pigs. Not that it bothered anyone, it was a fitting part of a farm.

Karl Lee went alone. No one in his family was interested in going with him this time. These trips were so frequent that there was nothing special about them any longer. Mari Lee said they could have dinner a little later that day so that he could eat with them. Said it with routine housewifely concern.

4

EVEN THOUGH IT WAS A WORKDAY people had a little extra time. That happened now and then, in between harvests. Old folks could sit and doze with their worn-out bodies. And youth had a chance to meet in the verdant groves.

Two such stepped out of the bushes at a spot where the road across the island went through the woods. It was Else and Rolf. They were both occupied with their own thoughts. A bit depressed. They sat down on the ground. Rolf lay flat on his back. Else sat beside him. She turned toward him, leaned on her elbow and stroked his arm and said, to feel him out:

'Dear Rolf.'

He pretended not to hear.

'Dear Rolf,' she could then say once more. She drew back and sat there, quiet and a little hurt. He could just lie there. –

He noticed it quickly, reached out and touched her and called softly to her:

'What's the matter, Else?'

'I'm so happy,' she answered.

Rolf was silent. That wasn't the way *he* felt just then. Not everything was easy and good. It was a big thing to be happy.

Else asked:

'Are you?'

'What?'

'Happy, of course.'

'Why do you ask like that?'

'Well, then, I won't ask. But *I'm* so happy. And so I think you must be, too, you see.'

He tried to smile:

'You say it so confidently.'

She looked at him uneasily.

'I say it as confidently as I can.'

He looked confused at that. Stood up and said as a pretext:

'Someone's coming. I think I heard footsteps.'

'No one's coming. You're so jumpy.'

'We're right in the middle of the road,' said Rolf.

'What difference does it make if someone comes?' she asked after a short pause. 'We can sit beside each other as much as we want, can't we?'

'Yes – ' he answered.

She was almost beside herself with all the doubt that had been eating at her lately. She looked into his face for signs.

'Isn't it for sure, then?' she asked. 'Isn't it serious?'

He drew her close to him and looked straight into her eyes as he said:

'*Is* it serious, Else?'

He was asking her to search herself. It grew lighter for her as she imagined she had found the answer.

'Yes,' she said. 'But then what's the matter?' she asked perplexed.

'It's just that we don't know how long it'll last,' answered Rolf.

'Yes, we do! Remember what you've said; remember what you said – '

He cut in:

'Oh, sure, you can say all sorts of things at times like that.'

She looked at him shocked.

'I don't understand you. Yes, I do, too; but – . Are you sorry for it, Rolf?'

'No, no. But it's so dangerous to promise something forever.'

'Why do you have such a bad conscience, anyway?' asked Else.

'Bad conscience?'

'Yes. What's happened there in town?'

He laughed impulsively, as if freed from something. Was on safe ground again.

'Nothing,' he replied. 'You'll just have to believe me.'

'Dear Rolf, I do want to believe you. It's so good when you're home.'

It sounded so true and sincere when she said it that it did him good. Good when you're home. He was only home during vacations.

He kissed her and said that it wouldn't be so many days before he was back at the grind again.

'Don't go!' she said.

'Don't go ? But I have to.'

'Oh, no, stop now that you're not enjoying it. I can tell that you're not, you know.'

'You don't know anything about it.'

'You've said you want to come back sometime. Stay here now and work the orchard.'

'Not yet!' he said hard and sharp. 'I want to learn more before I come back.'

She began to go.

'What are you going to do, Else ?'

'I have to go home and help get dinner – besides, I *want* to go home.'

'Wait then, I'll go with you. Don't get the wrong idea about this, Else.'

'I don't understand,' she said in confusion. 'You're so changeable that I'm all mixed up.'

He put his arms around her and told her not to talk like that. But she could not be calmed this time by just a caress:

'You swing back and forth. Your sister says so, too. It makes me feel so insecure.'

'What Inga says doesn't make any difference,' he said angrily. 'You don't have to drag my sister into it.'

He let her go.

'I think Inga probably knows you pretty well,' she said; 'you're not so easy to get along with, I guess.'

'Oh, you don't have to – '

'Now someone *is* coming,' Else interrupted. The gravel on the road crunched and they started, because they stood there quarreling. Felt guilty because they stood there and spoiled something.

A stranger came walking along the road, straight toward them.

So few people lived on the island that they quickly saw when someone did not belong there. It was a tall, well-dressed man approaching. He quickly came nearer and their attention was immediately drawn to his face. Fine features, but with something frightened and seeking over them. And the way he looked around: thirstingly, expectantly.

He had reached them.

They knew perfectly well that they should not just stare like that, but they could not help it. The man slowed down, looked at them, ready to say something, but said nothing after all.

They could not remember having seen such eyes as his. They were timid, but did not glide away. They were, on the contrary, searching. Searching for something to take part in; something unknown.

Looking into his eyes produced a strange effect. There was something at the breaking point in them.

He was quite a bit older than the twenty-year-olds he had met. He made them fear something they did not understand. It all lasted only a fleeting second. He did not stop to chat, or ask anything. His eyes glided away from them and fastened themselves on the landscape ahead. Now they saw only his back. He walked straight ahead.

They stood there and understood nothing. But they had clearly sensed something in his look that seemed to plead: help me.

How?

They had no way of knowing. They had been able to catch his wordless plea, but nothing more.

Else asked who that was.

Rolf just shook his head.

'He must be a long way from home. I think he even might have been a foreigner from his looks,' he said finally.

'Oh, not necessarily. – Rolf, I was almost afraid.'

'Afraid? What of?'

'He was so strange.'

She stood there and was small, and disturbed.

'Let's go.'

They began to go the same way the stranger had gone. Something about him drew them, and they offered no resistance.

They followed after him without even thinking about it. He had long since disappeared around the bend in the road.

5

IN A GROVE sat two older men. Their names were Hill and Dale and they had lived on the island all their lives. Worked there all their lives. They sat in the shade near the road. Something had happened that almost never happened: they had gotten hold of some beer and drunk a little too much of it. Yesterday they had worked hard. And tomorrow they'd go at it again. But today they thought they'd take a day off. They looked around, contented that the Lord had made this little holiday right in the middle of the week. The treacherous joy of beer had smoothed over the strange numbness that such a sudden day of leisure creates in a body used to working. They were free and at ease, they thought. As people certainly are meant to be.

They looked around. At their island. A cloudy mixture of joy and sorrow was stirred up in them.

Hill lifted his bottle of beer:

'Skoal for the island.'

Dale answered:

'Skoal. It's a good island.'

Then they realized that neither of them had any beer left. They were lifting empty bottles. They laughed, a little embarrassed at their childish behavior.

Hill threw his bottle aside.

Dale said apologetically:

'Oh, well – '

'Yep, it's all gone,' said Hill.

They felt it as a loss, and hung their heads. But then their clouded, stirred-up feelings settled out and became as clear spring water: their island. Theirs was a good island. It lay spread out before them. All their memories were connected with it and the surrounding waters. They had worked in the earth and fished in the sea all their lives.

Dale said:

'It's a good island even if the bottle is empty.'

'Yep.'

'So we can still say skoal for it.'

'Yep. We sure can.'

Their hands lay large and dead on each side of them. This green island *was* in such hands. Hands that were never allowed to become weary, or at least were never allowed to be at rest except for a few Sunday hours. Hill and Dale both had such hands. Tomorrow, when their tiny slip down into drunkenness had faded away – then their large, misshapen hands would be clenched around worn tool-handles and be more beautiful than angel hands.

They turned, because someone was coming along the road; they looked, and a look of annoyance came over their faces. They had sort of expected that something pleasing to look at would come along – just then as they were sitting there praising their island. A young girl or something like that.

But it was a tall, black-clad woman coming along the road. Kari Ness – who first had lost her husband at sea one stormy day, and then had lost two grown sons in another storm later. Now she was alone.

She had wandered and wandered around the island ever since. Black-clad. People did not like meeting her. They felt most like going off in another direction than they had intended if they saw her coming toward them at a distance. But she was not to be avoided.

Hill and Dale sat still and resigned themselves to her coming. Stared a little stupidly at her with their dull, drunken eyes.

She did not walk past. That was always the worst thing about her. It was as if she had made a pact with some power to disturb people, so that they could never forget what wretched dust they were. She came calling, whether welcome or not.

She stopped and spoke to them:

'Are you sitting here drinking?' she asked.

They cleared their throats and grunted a little in denial. Looked at her defiantly.

'No,' said Hill finally.

They were not drinkers and no more drunk than that they felt ashamed of themselves.

'I've been thinking,' said Kari Ness.

They did not answer. Just wished she would soon wander farther along the road and torment someone else. She was always doing that now. She was said to be not quite all right after what had happened to her.

But she would not leave.

'I've been asking,' she said.

'Oh,' said Dale, timidly.

She looked at them as if she wanted to add that she did not expect that *they* could help her in any way.

'But no one answers me,' she said.

She stood looking straight at them. What did she want?

'Yep, we thought we'd take today off,' said Hill suddenly. To defend his condition. He was troubled by her accusation that they were sitting there drinking beer.

He realized immediately that he should not have said that, either, for she looked at him coldly and began to walk away. She took long, stretching strides, as if she were setting out on a long trip. But she really only trudged around and around the island. Everyone met her constantly. She walked in a circle.

Look: long, thin, black legs stretching out, but yet getting nowhere. A shadow that appeared and frightened people again and again. Suddenly she stood there, tall and dark. If only she would move away from here and trouble our hearts no longer.

Hill and Dale heaved a sigh of relief when she disappeared around the bend in the road. They looked around for more beer, but in vain. The bottles lay empty and pointed here and there in the grass with their necks. And then Kari Ness. –

'Answer her? Oh, no,' said Dale.

'No, that's for the Lord to do, and not us,' replied Hill.

The gravel on the road crunched again and they turned to look with friendly eyes, for they were now at least sure that it was not Kari Ness.

A stranger came along. He was not from the island and they were glad for that. Before him they could just as well as not be a little tipsy, it made no difference. They could pump him about where he was going to their heart's content.

'Nowhere in particular,' he answered.

That shook them a bit. This was a weary and joyless man. And an answer they did not like. They hurried to say a lot of nonsense and told him that their names were Hill and Dale, but that they didn't care what his was.

He did not feel like standing there. Just went his way as if he were in a hurry.

'There's a strange one,' they said amazed and looked at his erect back.

'Have *you* seen him before?'

'No.'

'But he was a real man.'

'Yep, we were too, at one time.'

'Yep, there's nothing like real men. Skoal for the island.'

'We don't have any beer.'

They became silent again. Sat with their broad, open, workmen's hands rowing slowly at their sides.

6

THE YOUNG GIRL was still sitting on watch beside the pig pen. She sat bent over and motionless. Deep in thought. She was not particularly alert, but it was not necessary that she be, either. The sow brought her young into the world without difficulty; all went as it should. An eternal miracle, performed once more there in the crowded, ill-smelling pen. Creation. A thousand small things in order so that all could take place. Beyond comprehension. If Helga had thought about it seriously she would have grown faint at the thought. But she had other things to think about.

From up under the ceiling came the dull murmur of flies. Some were buzzing around, others sat as if asleep. And many hung grey with dust and lifeless in the spiderwebs.

From outside, from the open pens, came the soft grunting of all the little pigs. The boar sat and yawned, marooned in a desert of boredom.

But inside, the miracle of life was taking place.

Suddenly the whole picture changed.

Jens, the owner of the pigs, walked toward the barn with a 'clipper' as he was called; a man who travelled around on the islands and castrated new-born pigs. He wore a white jacket but it was doubtful if he was a fully-trained veterinarian. But Jens had sent for him this time, as every time before when he had had small pigs to be treated. It was not an especially pleasant business, but unavoidable for a pig-raiser.

The two men stood beside the pens where the tiny pigs were tumbling about. The man in the white jacket picked through the pile. Among the sons there. Just as a beginning, a survey. All the tiny sons and daughters lay mixed together in a pile. They slept, or looked at the man with their watery blue eyes.

B

The sows rolled over and grew restless. As if they recognized the man. They pulled themselves to their feet and stood there, grey with mud and heavy. Threatening and large, and silent. Each in her separate pen.

But it appeared to pass over. Food came into the troughs and the sucked-out sows were starved. They went to their troughs and let their young crawl about as they pleased. Just as on any other day. Except that the food was better than usual. They buried their snouts in it.

The boar, over in his wasteland, was given nothing. It was not yet feeding time. But he had good ears, and heard how the sows ate. He let them know what he thought about it. All who were near jumped, and the sows stopped eating. But not for long, they were soon chewing and chomping again. And the boar got no food. He shoved his snout under a loose stone and threw it into the air. The stone fell back down onto his skull. Into the hollow pit beneath the overhanging brow. Thud – into the dark pit. It did not put him in any better mood.

But it was not he, it was the tiny pink pigs that were of importance this morning. They were shut off from their mothers. One by one the sons were picked out. They squealed as they were lifted out of the pile. It sounded like the whining of a tiny saw.

A heavy, dark mist descended over it all.

The baby pigs were restless. Their mother was gone. They whined.

Inside the barn, sitting with the youngest sow, the girl began to listen. The sounds sent small waves of tension through her. The youngest sow was struggling to give birth, but heard, and grew uneasy. Every now and then she started.

The small squeals also caused the sows at the troughs to stop chomping. They listened. They were in separate pens, and the pens were locked. They lost their appetites, and listened tensely.

It grew dark about them. The pits in their brows deepened. Their eyes clouded over. They looked at each other through the cracks in the board fence that separated their pens.

A small squeal rose up – then silence again –

A bellow mixed with it – from outside. From the boar. He listened, also tensed and on edge.

Inside, Helga counted the new litter. There were many. Now there was rest after the struggle; but also nervous listening to what was happening outside.

A tiny saw whined again.

The sows heard it. Tensed. Their senses clouded.

Thud –

Not from outside, as when the boar was struck by the stone, but from inside.

Thud – down into the abyss. To the doomed and lost. Into the dark pit. A glimpse there. Then it flamed up. Ignited by a squeal. It came over them both simultaneously, so that it would be impossible to point out one as the origin. The spark leaped between them with no loss of time. Each saw the other as a deadly enemy. There was no time to think about why it was so. They had both heard the whine. Had both seen each other through the cracks in the fence. It could not be forgiven.

The board fence between them was no more than a wall of cardboard when they charged it and splintered it with quick, sharp blows of their heads. The pieces of broken board flew to all sides and they struck at each other in blind rage.

It just happened. –

The other must be destroyed – for having been a witness to something forbidden.

Now it could be seen that they were not just blubber. In their compressed brains plans of attack awakened alongside of meaningless rage. Tusks glistened, in vicious sidewise chops of the head. A blow with the snout – and the enemy should lie there torn to pieces. It had been like that in the jungle at one time, in the dimness far back in the family.

But there was no such devastating rending of the enemy here.

The enemy sensed the blow and countered it. Tusks clashed together and tore at the surface fat and into the meat. Just external wounds that only increased their rage and strength. They became filled with a living wildness. All their dead calm was thrown aside, as if it were a mask – revealing itself as dangerous energy and power.

Perhaps the small squeals continued, but they were drowned out by the roaring of the sows.

Their bellows were now and then augmented by the sound of splintering wood and the grunt each time their bedevilled bodies collided.

The boar in his solitude started up. He recognized their voices. At first he was struck by a spark of their insanity, and charged at his fence with a roar. The dry wood splintered a little and became white and pure inside the coating of mud. But his pen was extra-strongly built and the planks held. The fence was so high that he could not get over it. The wild beast in him was awakened and his lank body was seized by convulsions. But he could not get over the fence.

Only the first roars on the other side of the fence had this effect on him. After the tumult increased the boar was stricken with fear. He was seized by a numbing fear and fell in a heap in the mud. He listened between each breath and felt that dangerous things were approaching in these screams. He was paralyzed. He opened his jaws to bellow, but no sound came out. In the darkness in his brow his thoughts lay tangled and entwined. He was for the time being finished, and put out of action.

But the sows were not so quickly finished. They were still flying at each other in full rage. The other must be destroyed. The reason was long since forgotten. Blood flowed freely from the tusk wounds. Their bellows filled the air.

The two men had quickly stopped working. They raced around the pen and shouted to each other in confusion. But they could do nothing. It was impossible to go in and try to separate the two raging sows. Helga had come out. And Bergit, Jens' wife. The sows knew her and were fond of her, but not at this moment. They all ran back and forth and shouted to each other:

'Get a gun – '

'Yes, shoot one of them – '

'No, no,' cried Bergit. 'Not now when they have so many young to raise.'

'But they'll kill each other – '

'No, no – '

The baby pigs lay in a pile in a corner. They had ducked down, and lay there unmoving. Something in them had forced them into this position. The danger. The tumult. Something incomprehensible. They ducked down and lay still.

A crash. The pen gave way under a heavy side blow. The sows tumbled out into the barnyard and headed for the people standing there. They attacked the people – at the same time that they were fighting with each other to the death and gashing each other's sides. They attacked everything that moved.

The two men and the woman ran for the house. The girl slipped back into the barn.

But the devil was in the sows now. No sooner had the people begun to collect themselves a bit behind the closed door of the tidy house than the door flew open. They had not thought to lock it, and the door opened inwards. The sows were suddenly there and stuck their bloody snouts through the door. They stopped and stood still an instant to take aim.

The effect of this sight on the three people in the room was paralyzing. An instant of fear. Wild beasts. Demons.

What was it? What would happen?

Nothing! It was only the two sows that Bergit carried food to many times a day! No; they were transformed. They were something else. Bestiality itself stuck its snout into human life: dark, filthy and consuming.

A second: – The devil is visiting our house. Prepare yourself, you who shall be led away – they did not know what thoughts and feelings were racing through them. But those brutal, bloody snouts were there right in front of them.

A second. Then Jens came to life. He grabbed a small bench and threw it at the sows with all his might.

'Out!' he managed to shout at them.

The sows had not expected that. They squealed, turned and ran back out into the yard.

The room was cleared. The sight was gone. Now it was only the two familiar sows, but they were enraged and were racing to their doom.

They must not kill each other! They were valuable animals that must be caught before it was too late. Jens and Bergit and the 'clipper' found sticks and ran out into the barnyard again. Bergit also took along a pail of food, to coax them with.

The battle was still raging. Blindly. Neither gave up. They charged and gashed each other. Then staggered back. Helga had left the youngest sow again and hung out of a window.

'Watch out,' Bergit screamed. 'The well!'

'The well! Get them away from it!'

Too late. There was an old well beside the barn. Useless, deep, empty, but not filled in – there were only grown-ups on the farm, so it was not dangerous for anyone. The edge was rotten and crumbled and even with the ground, with only bits of rubbish around it. The sows tumbled right into it. The first fell in with a squeal and the other was so close on her heels that she could not stop, but tumbled in after. Away from the face of the earth in a flash, both of them.

The three people heard only a fleshy thump when the second sow struck the first down in the dry well. They ran over to the opening. The animals lay there far below with broken necks. They kicked a little and died, their bodies twisted. They glistened faintly, grey-white, deep down in the earth.

They turned quickly. No one had noticed that Helga had jumped down from the window, but now they heard her shouting in fear from inside the barn:

'Help!'

'What now?'

They ran. A strange sound came out through the door. Wasn't it over yet?

The girl screamed again:

'Help! Come here. She's eating them!'

Of course. She was eating them.

'She's eating her young.'

They said it in unison.

'Of course. I should have known – in all this racket. They can't stand it.'

They ran into the barn. Two doors opened into the room. They saw in passing that a man was standing in the other door. Standing there with staring eyes. But they had no time to worry about him for the time being. Helga had not seen him. They all had eyes only for the youngest sow. She had turned on her litter of young, with a strange growling, throaty sound. She was gulping down her young, eating them. Her body was seized by rapid, irregular convulsions.

They stood still an instant, staring in horror.

It's here.

The abyss is here.

'Get them away!' shouted the woman to her daughter before she could reach them herself.

Helga had managed to brush a few aside, but now she just stood there at a loss for what to do. The sow ate with terrifying speed, driven insane by the shock of all she had heard out in the yard.

Jens got there first, and saved a few more of the baby pigs. His hands were shaking. It was like being deep, deep down somewhere. Beneath the green earth. Among the bedevilled.

Wasn't there a man standing in the door there before? He was not there now. He had fled.

7

YES, HE HAD FLED. Andreas West.

Something had snapped inside his brain. A puff of evil light, and then no more. Darkness. Everything was just as before, to all appearances, but irreparable things had happened deep below the surface. – And he fled from Lee.

Into the bushes. Just away. Into the groves, into the thick lattice-work of leaves of the underbrush on that fertile patch of earth.

What was he going to do there?

Lie there in wait, he thought. In there and lie in wait, in case something came along that was for him. No, not that either. He didn't know. New, uncontrollable thoughts raged in his brain in the wake of the hidden breakdown.

He did not break a twig, but ran lightly and soundlessly.

The voice had called to him so promisingly as he walked across the island. He had met people, but had not tried to come in contact with them. Not yet. First he had to walk and walk by himself, and listen to the calling from this fertile patch of earth, from this new peace:

Andreas!

A voice within him answered:

Yes, it's here I'll be healed. Here I'll find peace and, best of all, here I'll forget.

So maybe fate is kind to me compared to others I've seen. To all those who were burned and consumed in the explosion, he thought.

Watch yourself – don't think about that. Look, your hands are shaking.

Yes, because it's calling to me here.

He walked out of the woods and onto a meadow that was dark green with hay. The meadow was wide and green for the second time.

33

Up on a hill lay a farm. With a huge dark red barn, its roof crowned by the leaves of surrounding trees. It was beautiful, and neat and tidy looking.

He followed the road up to the farm. The road went in a wide arc up the hill, to make it as easy as possible for a horse to bring the harvest in. There was not a sound to be heard from up there.

He started:

Do you remember ? –

There they were again. The memories. But at the moment he was able to shut them in. The tempting voice said so gently and so softly: Andreas, come to me, I am watching over you –

He trembled, and believed.

He neared the farm buildings. Now that he had gained some height he had a view over the island and the sea. His agonized heart throbbed with joy at the sight.

'Yes,' he said, aloud.

Then he walked on up the hill.

He started violently. Had heard some shrill screams from up at the farm. What was that? The screams died away before they got beyond the limits of the barnyard, but were sharp and penetrating. A chill gripped him. But then he got hold of himself: It's just some animals. Pigs. I've heard squealing and screeching like that before. It's nothing.

It passed over quickly.

He continued toward the farm. But he was not fully as calm as before, for the sounds grew louder as he approached. Squealing and bellowing. Ugly.

He calmed himself: It's only some animals acting up. For some reason that I don't understand. I don't know much about farms and animals. There – now it's stopped.

Suddenly it was quiet. He had reached the barn. A thrill of joy ran through him at the sight of the red barn and the broad orchard below it. The right kind of people live here, he thought. I can see that even if I know nothing about farming.

He could not see the barnyard, it was ringed in by buildings. The road turned at the corner of the barn. Just then a frightened cry came from inside the barn:

'Help!'

He heard a woman's voice, penetrating:

'Come here! She's eating them!'

'She's eating them,' came the answer farther away.

He did not understand what it meant, nor did he think about it, either. He only heard the cry for help and his body obeyed automatically.

In, and see if I can help somehow.

The cry came from within the barn beside him and there was a door near where he stood. It was open. He ran in. He was met by a sour smell. Dust-grey flies flew up into his face.

The cry came from a pen in a corner, and a young girl was struggling to gather something up from the straw in it.

He stepped forward. The girl was so excited that she did not even notice him. But he was no longer looking at her either. His eyes grew large at what he saw in the pen:

A grunting sow was eating her young. Ravenously. Blindly.

He felt like screaming, but stood there stiffly instead and could make no sound at all. The sight was too much for him.

Look. A mother eating her children.

Look at life. A mother chewing her child. Child after child. At the mouth of a yawning abyss. Why?

The senseless sight before him caused his over-strained nerves to give way entirely. That sight in the barn was the last touch needed to complete his destruction. His half-crazed mind could stand no more.

Something snapped, and blazed up, and it was over. A shock ran through him as his reason burned up.

He regained his normal appearance.

He remained standing there a little while. Someone came rushing in, a couple of men who began digging frantically in the pen. He backed out the door he had come through and quietly ran away.

The trembling inside him was gone.

He ran quietly away. Back down the road. Off the road and into the thick bushes. The bushes brushed gently against his cheek and brow. It brought a beautiful smile to his face.

'What ?' he said and turned around.

There was no one following him.

He ran quietly and lightly on.

8

ELSE AND ROLF HAD PARTED. At first they followed the stranger along the road. Just because the meeting with him had affected them like that. Then they slowed down. Else said that she just had to go home and help with dinner.

'All right,' answered Rolf shortly.

The stranger had disappeared, and his effect was gone. They were left standing there with their own problems – under the trees that arched over the road. Something near them smelled strong and over-ripe.

Else said:

'Sometimes I'm sure you'd like to be rid of me.'

'Nonsense.'

'I can't understand it any other way. I've so many little examples.'

'That you go out of your way to collect.'

'Well, I have to. They mean a lot, you know.'

'You shouldn't have such exaggerated ideas about what all this means,' said Rolf. 'That's what it is. Then you wouldn't go making demands for things that are beyond human power.'

He was fully aware that it was unkind to say that. But he had needed to say it.

It hit Else hard, he saw that. But he wanted to have it said. He was so mixed up about it all.

'I think it would be best for me not to talk to you any more to-day,' Else said. 'Then you won't have to say any more stupid things.'

'Maybe so.'

'Yes, I think that's safer. Thanks for the walk, Rolf.'

'All the same ?'

Stupid, she had said. That little word made him angry. Which was why he had said 'all the same' so bitingly.

But she would not let herself be tempted to retort with new insults. She said only:

'Yes, all the same.'

She said it in a friendly way and grew by it.

'So long,' he said.

She turned to go home along one of the many side roads that ran through the fields and groves across the island. Rolf took another side road that led to Lee.

He looked back. Sure enough: there she stood. Looking to see if he would follow her.

He hurried along and kicked at a puff ball at the edge of the road. It exploded. Then he walked quickly and got out of her sight.

He walked along without looking or hearing. Around him the leaves moved slightly, and the forest grass. Wind from the sea. Then nothing more. Everything became sleepy again. Broiling hot, and still. And the sun was not yet at its highest. It was hard to breathe. Rolf drew in the heavy air and felt even more out of sorts and confused.

Girls, he thought.

If only there were none!

Oh no, but if only they were as they *should* be.

That stranger, he thought suddenly – just how was it he looked at you, anyway ? What was it that made you follow him with such longing ?

The bushes in front of him began quivering. A girl stepped onto the path with a couple of long green plants in her hand. She herself was tall and young.

Rolf stared at her. At his sister. Inga. Seventeen.

She turned her back to him. She was probably looking for new plants. She was always looking for new plants, and seemed to find them, too. He called to her:

'Inga.'

She answered without turning around. So she must have already seen him.

'Yes, do you want something?'

'No.'

He went up to her.

'What are you doing with those weeds?'

She continued searching through the bushes, without turning around.

'You're a weed – what are you doing snooping around here for, anyway?' she answered in a friendly tone. She had always been a good friend, both at play and at work in the orchard.

He stood close beside her. Looked at her. She did not look happy. It struck him how little happy she looked.

'What's wrong, Inga?'

'Wrong? What do you mean?'

She looked almost angrily at her brother. As if he irritated her.

'It's so hot!' he said. 'You can hardly breathe in this sticky weather.'

'Oh, sure you can. But you're in a bad mood today again. I can see that.'

'Am I?'

'Yes, and much too often, too. It's about time you got over that, Rolf.'

' 'Cause I'm a big boy now,' he mimicked. 'Isn't that how it goes?'

She laughed.

'Yes, that's what parents say.'

He stood looking at her. She was tall and thin. He liked her. They had always been together.

'Where are you going?' he asked.

She had already started off.

'Mother's over here,' she answered. 'We went for a walk together. She's taken a nice long walk today, too, since there was time for it. I just ran over here to pick these weeds.'

She walked away.

9

INGA REJOINED HER MOTHER.

Mari Lee had sat down on a stone and waited for her. Inga saw her familiar back, slightly rounded after long years of hard work, but not worn out. Thoroughly and honestly weary, but still able to bear the burden of many days. A housewife's back.

The sea could be seen through an opening in the leaves, and Mari Lee sat facing this opening. She sat unmoving, recognized the footsteps of her daughter, and said without turning around:

'You were quite a while –'

'Oh, yes.'

'Well, it was good just to sit here, it's not often I get a chance. I've been sitting here and waiting for a breath of wind through that opening in the leaves, but today there's not even a breath from the sea.'

'No.'

Mari Lee turned at this absent-minded answer from her daughter. Inga asked:

'What's the matter?'

'Nothing. There's hardly a sound out of you today.'

Inga laughed.

'Oh, sure there is. The heat just makes me so dull.'

'Yes, it's strenuous when it's so hot day after day. And when you have to stand over a hot stove as well. We'd better go home and get dinner.'

'Oh, we don't have to think about dinner for a long time yet. Dad's not back yet and we got some of it ready before we left.'

'Rolf will be hungry,' Mari Lee answered out of habit and the long experience of a boy's growing up.

'Oh, Rolf can take care of himself as well as anybody else.'

'Isn't it strange: just because it's a workday you can't really enjoy sitting here as we're doing. You sit and feel that you're wasting time. It must be wrong to have worked so hard that you feel like that.'

Inga said nothing.

'No, you know nothing about that yet,' her mother continued. 'But it comes, gradually. If you sit down, you feel guilty. It's probably that way on every farm.'

'Oh, that's just nonsense!' said Inga.

Her mother was a bit taken aback at her hostile tone of voice. She had a large, pleasant face. Now as she spoke, many weary lines came over it. She asked quickly:

'What's the matter, Inga?'

'Nothing. I've told you that.'

Her evasive manner made her mother sigh. An often used sigh; that was easy to hear.

'What's bothering you all the time now, Inga? I understand so little about you now. You're so often cross when we can't feel it's our fault.'

They looked at each other. Their faces were identical, feature for feature. But the one was tensed and expectant, the other a bit sad, and weary. Inga saw this and asked quickly, frightened:

'Doesn't it work out with the things you think about when you're my age?'

'With the things you think about?'

'Yes, you think about so many things. At least, I do. And others do, too. Things you're going to be a part of, and get. You must have done it, too. But now you're tired and unhappy.'

Her mother took it as some sort of accusation, so that she felt that she had to defend herself somehow.

'I don't understand you,' she said. 'We weren't like that when I was young.'

'Oh, sure, you were. You thought about getting all sorts of things, too!'

'All sorts of things? I have both you and Rolf.'

Inga became confused and small at that. She had no reply.

'So I feel I've had enough,' her mother continued. 'But now it's slipping away from me. That's what wears you out.'

Inga was still at a loss for something to say. Her mother came with *her* accusation:

'You talk less and less to me about what you have on your hearts.'

'No, we don't either!' Inga cried out. 'Yes, I guess we do. I'm sorry, mother, but we just can't.'

'Why not?'

'Well, it's just always like that, you know.'

'Yes, I know.'

She said it in resignation. They sat there side by side, each with her own thoughts, looking through the opening in the leaves at the quiet sea. Then Mari Lee said suddenly:

'I have so many memories of you and Rolf that it seems there are as many as there are leaves on the trees.'

Her voice was charged with so much of that which she saw before her that it was as if it had touched a string in her that had sung in response.

Inga could say nothing again. She knew that her mother was speaking the truth. About all that she had had. But what had happened then? It was obvious that something had happened, that her mother had suffered disappointment.

For Inga the words called forth bursts of concentrated memories of their years together. From her childhood on, inseparably bound to the constant work in the large orchard and to the quiet winters in

the house. Her mother, who had cared for and worried about it all,
and behind of her stood her father, Karl Lee, even more at one
with the orchard and the work outside. Her father always rose up
before her large and serious when she thought of him. The picture
was immutable.

'Look at your father!' her mother had said one time she could
remember clearly.

Look at him? Why? He had been working among the myriad of
fruit trees. Rolf and she had just stood there and stared.

'Don't you see how he works,' their mother had said. 'I do.'

'Works?'

'Yes, it won't be long now before you'll have to go at it more in
earnest, both of you. He expects it, you know.'

A thought struck them: is that why he's so strict?

They had gone from their mother with little joy in their hearts
that time. But not long after they had begun to work in the orchard.
And they had not been lazy, either. But then Rolf had left. They saw
him only a few short weeks during the year. He had become so
difficult and unrecognizable of late.

Mari Lee stood up.

'Well, I'm going home and tend to dinner. You can come along
later.'

'Oh, no, I'll come with you, of course. I just said there was no
rush.'

'I don't like waiting until the last minute, you know that. Phew,
it's hot,' she concluded, and stretched.

They heard a shout from over at the road. A woman stood there
waving her hand. Inga recognized her immediately.

'Look, there's Gudrun. What do you want?' she called over.
'Come on over here.'

'Yes, and for once her husband's not with her,' said Mari Lee and
waited idly. Gudrun was so near that she had to say the few words
required of her before it would be polite to leave. She knew it was
Inga the woman was looking for, not her.

Gudrun came running over and greeted them gaily. She had only recently married a teacher on the island and was one of Inga's best friends, even though she was several years older.

'I was up at the farm looking for you, Inga, but only Bergit and Jens were home.'

'Well, I was just about to head up that way,' said Mari Lee. 'We sneaked away from the stove for a few minutes. But where's your husband today, Gudrun ? We hardly ever see just one of you.'

Gudrun laughed happily.

'Oh, we've been married longer than that,' she said. 'It doesn't take so long.'

'Well, come along with us then. Or when you two have finished talking. You can have dinner with us.'

The two girls heard it clearly: when you two have finished talking. The older woman did not feel included. But that could not be helped.

'Thank you,' replied Gudrun, 'but *my* husband has to have dinner, too. I just wanted to talk – '

'Yes, of course.'

The few required words were said. Mari Lee could go now. It was easy to read in Gudrun's face that she had important news. But not for me. We who are old aren't let in on their secrets.

She kicked at a twig that lay on the path.

10

INGA COULD ALSO SEE that Gudrun had something important to tell her.

'What is it, Gudrun ?'

Gudrun did not answer.

'Come on. I can see there's something.'

A strange, happy sound tumbled out of Gudrun as she answered:
'It's just about everything!' she said.

'Oh, don't be silly; what is it?'

'Of course it's only one thing, but it's still everything. I'm going to have a baby – '

'No, not really!'

'Yes. I've thought so a long time now, but I haven't told it to anyone, except Ivar. But I just can't keep quiet any longer now!'

Inga was deeply moved by the news. Gudrun bubbled on. Many different feelings rose up in Inga. Her older friend seemed to grow before her eyes and become mighty.

'Just think – ' was all she could say.

'When will it be?' she asked suddenly.

'Early in the spring sometime. Everything will be like new now.'

'Will it? Yes, of course it will. Aren't you a bit afraid, too?'

'Afraid? No – I don't think there's anything to be afraid of.'

Inga stood there and saw how Gudrun shone. She thought about what was happening inside her.

'What does Ivar say about it? What did he say?'

'He said I'd get a little prize. Oh, him – he doesn't make any difference now.'

'What!'

Gudrun had said a bit too much.

'Oh, no, it's silly of me to say that, but don't you see that everything else means nothing to me now?'

'Yes – '

'There's just one thing now.'

'You told *me* first,' Inga said proudly, without ever thinking about how childish she was being.

'Oh, well – you know, I'm just busting to tell it. Can you understand that something like this should be kept secret as long as possible? What nonsense! That I should live here among people who know nothing about it. I'd like to tell it to the four winds.'

Inga just said about it all:

'Oh, how wonderful! – just to hear about it is like – '

'Yes, for me,' said Gudrun, and drew a boundary between them.

Inga felt it clearly enough. A little shadow of poverty crossed her face: the thought of the great difference between them now.

'Oh, sure, it's you it's wonderful for, but – '

'I've got to go now,' interrupted Gudrun, and had already started off.

'Oh, no, don't go,' said the half-grown, lonely, poor, dream-filled girl.

Gudrun in her wealth saw nothing of it all. She was much too rich.

'I just wanted to come and tell you, and then run home again.'

'Sure.'

'For nothing to compare to this will ever happen to me again!'

An exultant cry.

'I know,' said Inga. 'Gudrun,' she added quickly, 'aren't you afraid at all?'

'No. But I've got to go now. And – keep it to yourself, will you? So far we're the only ones who know about it.'

'Sure, and come again soon.'

'*You* come,' Gudrun called back as she began to run off. Then she stopped:

'Well, maybe just a little bit.'

'Afraid?'

'Yes.'

'Sure you are.'

'But that's all right.'

Then she turned and ran.

Inga was left standing there. Early in the spring sometime, she thought. She stood there without moving, and thought about men. I'll have a baby sometime, too.

That's not so certain.

Oh, yes, no one can deny me that! she thought defiantly.

11

INGA DID NOT KNOW how long she had been standing there like that. Overwhelmed. Then she began to go. In her hand she still held the long, flowerless plants. Overwhelmed by visions of the future.

A thick wall of leaves grew beside the path. Inga let her eyes sweep along it as she walked. Suddenly she started, stopped and cried out: 'Gudrun!'

A foolish cry. Gudrun was by then far out of earshot and could not come to help her. A plea for help lay hidden in her cry.

No answer. She could not summon help.

Run! a voice inside her seemed to command, but though she wanted to, her feet would not obey. Her feet were paralyzed. Not to be moved. She stared at a spot in the wall of leaves beside the road.

She saw an eye in there. Nothing but an eye that seemed to send out a paralyzing beam. She easily recognized it as a man's eye. Turned toward her. Toward her eyes. Nothing moved. Only an eye stared at her and held her fast.

Help me, she thought instinctively. She sensed danger.

She wished so intensely for help that she felt she had been given it, been given so much courage that she could lift her arm and point at the leaves and call out:

'Who's there?'

Nothing moved.

'Who's in there?' she asked, in deep need and fear.

Nothing moved. No answer.

'Come out!' she shouted. 'Let me see you!'

That had an immediate effect. The leaves began quivering. The bushes were parted by a man's hand. A man stepped out onto the road. A handsome, well-dressed man. A stranger. Inga's fear fell away. She felt a great relief. What in the world had she thought was in there, anyway? She had no idea. Sudden, silly whims. She sighed deeply. Then she saw that the stranger had probably not seen her yet, the way he was behaving.

He had stepped onto the road with his back to her and started to walk away. As if he had never seen her. He said out loud to no one:

'No, I've never seen anything like – '

'What ?' said Inga impulsively, unintentionally.

Then the man saw her. He turned abruptly and looked at her. His eyes shone with a strange light. An alien streaming. It never occurred to Inga that it was insanity. That the sense of reason behind those eyes had burned up. They were placed in such a handsome face.

The man made a gesture of having suddenly become aware of her and asked politely:

'Pardon me, did you say something to me ?'

'No, I just – ' Inga said, flustered. 'No, it was nothing. I just said – '

The man smiled charmingly.

'And I guess I said that I've never seen so green an island before, and that's true. I can't remember ever having seen anything so fertile.'

Inga felt relieved and happy, freed of her shock. She stood there holding the long plants in her hand. She made herself as pretty as she could and asked:

'Haven't you ever been here before ?'

She thought: he can see I'm pretty. He saw it right away. What was he doing standing in that grove ? Well, he has a right to if he wants to. It was silly of me to be afraid like that.

She stood still and let the long plants swing slowly back and forth like a pendulum beside her knee. He noticed the plants.

'No, I've never been here before,' he said. 'But I can see that was stupid of me. I'm collecting plants and I've never seen so many different kinds in one place as here.'

Inga said happily:

'Oh! Do you collect plants ?'

She thought: we have the same interests. –

His crazed eyes had quickly noticed the plants. His brain had immediately sensed an easy and sure plan. Quick as lightning.

'Yes, I collect plants,' he said, 'and I've already seen a lot here that are new for me and that I'll make sure to get later. Do you get the same joy from them as I do?'

'The same joy?'

It was not because she did not understand what he meant that she repeated his words, it was just so good to do so. She was entranced by that strange light in his eyes, that gleaming that she did not understand. But it was so beautiful – he was so fine to look at that everything about him must be beautiful, she thought.

He said, as he pointed at the plants that brushed against her knee:

'I can see that you get the same joy from finding rare plants. You must be happy living in a place like this.'

It was wonderful to listen to him.

'Yes, I am,' she replied.

And I *am*! she said to herself. I've always been happy here.

'I can see that you can really find rare plants here, too,' he continued.

'If I only had more time to search over the whole island and look for them! I just got here.'

'Oh; you just got here. Then you've not had a chance to see much of what we have here.'

'Oh? Maybe not –'

'No, I'm sure you haven't. But you should have come earlier. It's so late in the summer now.'

He replied only:

'The worst of it is that I've got to leave again right away. I can't stay now.'

'Oh, please do!' burst out of her.

He just shook his head.

'My boat is waiting down at the dock. I just don't have time today. I've finished my errand here.'

He mustn't go, she thought.

'Goodbye,' he said and nodded. 'I'll really have to try to come again sometime. But I'm not sure I'll be able to.'

He started to leave. He took his time, but she did not notice that.

He mustn't leave as soon as I've met him, she thought.

'Can't that boat wait just a little bit ?' she pleaded.

'Oh, no,' he answered. 'It's not worth it. It's not only the boat; I just don't have the time, either.'

She thought of something:

'But let me just show you a couple of plants right close by here at least. It won't take long. I know right where they are.'

'Thanks, but I may have already seen them, and anyway – well, goodbye, then.'

'You haven't seen them!' she said eagerly. 'I'm positive. You have to know your way around here to find them. They're under a little cliff.'

'Thanks, but – '

'You've just got to see them! It's people like you who should see them. Nobody on the whole island cares anything about them except me, that's why it's so important. I've never met anyone before who was interested in such things.'

That's true, she said to herself, and I've just got to see more of him, too. Yes, I guess it's mostly that. Can't he see how pretty I am any longer ? Dosn't it do anything to him ? What can I do to make him see it, so that he'll stay ?

He listened to her words. His burnt-out brain was working rapidly and precisely. He had grasped his chance. Knew just what to do. Did it quickly and surely.

'Well, I can't resist that,' he said and let his face shine at her so that she stood there blind and happy.

'Oh, that's fine,' she replied, her voice soft and full of thanks.

'That boat'll have to wait a quarter of an hour or so. Will it take any longer ?'

A quarter of an hour ? So little time! she thought. She answered:

'Oh, no. It's right here nearby. But it's so hidden away at the same time.'

He nodded.

'That's right,' he said. 'That kind of plant always grows in such places. Is this the way?'

'No, this way. Over here.'

They began to go. Now I'm walking beside him, she thought. Her heart was pounding.

Andreas West – ?

No, the calling was no longer there. Dark, incognizable thoughts raced through his mind – and flared up in there like a white flame and showed him what he had to do, had to say. He did not need to hesitate a second. And among the flames raced strange feelings like a dark stream through jagged gullies and gorges. Uncontrollably strong. This young girl was doomed.

She spoke, filled with joy over what was happening and converting it into love for this green island that had rare plants to offer:

'I've lived all my life on this island. I was born and raised here.'

'Then you must be happy,' he said. 'I can't understand that a person wouldn't be.'

Happy, he had said. Wasn't that the second time he had used that word? Yes, she was happy. She looked back over her life and it seemed that she had always been happy. She understood it now.

They walked along the road together. Inga said suddenly:

'But I had a fright when I saw you in the bushes! I thought you were just standing still in there. I thought I saw an eye and nothing more.'

He laughed gently.

'Of course I had to stand still,' he said. 'All of a sudden I saw you and I stood still.'

I'm happy, she thought.

'We have to head off the path here,' she said, as if she had not heard him. 'Down through the woods. They're under a little cliff.'

They stepped into the woods. The leaves closed behind them.

12

THE ROAD WAS EMPTY for perhaps a minute. Then the same bushes parted and Kari Ness stepped out. Dark-clad, deep in thought. She was both here and not here. She created an oppressive silence by stopping on the road and standing there like a statue.

After a moment of thought she turned toward the woods she had just stepped out of and said:

'Not a sparrow falls to earth but that it is the will of God.'

She stood still and seemed to be listening to see if anyone denied or affirmed it. Kari Ness –

No answer came. She let her own voice fill the deadly silence with short, broken sentences:

'Not a sparrow – '

'But can it be – '

'He who has faith but as a seed of mustard!' she concluded in a sharp, penetrating voice.

Hill and Dale came lurching through a grove in the woods. They had gotten over the first touch of shame at their little spree and walked along freely, each with a handful of empty beer bottles. Hill said in a happy voice:

'Sure is hard to get out of this here grove.'

'Yep,' said Dale. 'Skoal for the island and everything on it.'

'Say,' said Hill suddenly, 'Ivar's wife's gonna have a baby.'

'Gudrun?'

'That's what I've heard.'

They started at something they heard behind them somewhere among the leaves, close by. A voice said loud and clear:

'God help me to have faith.'

A chill ran down their spines and they looked at each other.

'What was that?'

'Must be Kari Ness.'

'Sure, must be her. We can never get rid of her.'

They looked around for her, for that clear voice that disturbed them. They could not see her for the leaves that separated them.

They groped around a bit.

'What'll we do with her?'

'With Kari Ness?'

'Yes, we've got to get rid of her somehow.'

They tried to clear their minds so that they could think of something. Her voice had cut through the beery fog enveloping their thoughts.

'Yep, we've got to get rid of her, but – '

They could find no solution to the problem right then, and had to lay it aside.

Rolf wandered about impatiently. He had unbuttoned his shirt, but it was just as stifling as before. Inga had left him to find Mother. He was just wandering back and forth.

I can't stand lying to Else any longer, he was thinking. She can see I'm lying, anyway.

He stopped suddenly. Had run straight into Hill and Dale when he rounded a bush. He had almost bumped into Hill's friendly, drunken face.

'Hey, boy!' they said. 'You walking around in a cloud?'

They were going to say more, but suddenly grew silent. Rolf also grew silent.

'Look, there she is.'

They saw Kari Ness. She did not see them, hidden as they were. She stood looking in another direction, as if she had seen something there, and her voice sounded again, and stopped their breathing:

'But I'm so terribly afraid – '

They stood still. Just stood, stood listening and waiting for more. An incomprehensible, breathless waiting – what was – ?

What was that? Just after Kari Ness' voice had died away something fell like a large, dark screen over the earth. Like a huge, black, distended and fragile blossom. It struck the ground and was gone. It was a cry.

Everyone in the vicinity looked up in confusion, and listened. Jumped up and stood still. Numb, listening for more sounds. But only that one great cry came.

A penetrating cry that unfolded itself and fell to earth and shattered around them like a dark film. Like a second of twilight in the middle of the day.

Out of the leaves came the voice of Kari Ness, despairing and lonely and knowing:

'Inga has left us!'

From another spot came the sound of a double male voice through the breathless silence: Hill and Dale had also sensed it.

'Murder!'

The word sounded through the woods to all who were near. There were people everywhere, on the paths and roads and on the nearby farms. The word was said, and became so living and tangible that it was as if a real being had risen up from the earth. Murder itself. In human form. And stood there with a leer on its face.

Everyone saw it. Everyone who had heard the word as it was thrown out. They did not actually see it, but felt it and let it take form.

Life came back to them. Hill and Dale and Rolf, or someone, shouted:

'Find him!'

It took hold. The cry had come from close by and they stormed off to the aid of whomever it was who had cried out in need. Into the bushes. People came running from all directions.

They found the dead girl. There was nothing that could be done. Then they bumped into a stranger who came rushing blindly out of their midst and past them and away.

They felt immediately that it was the murderer, and were infected by his speed.

'There he is! Stop him! Catch him!'

Someone took charge of the dead girl. Hill and Dale. They were not drunk any longer.

The others ran off. With Rolf at their head. Kari Ness had left; she was at any rate no longer to be seen.

Inga –

A wild rage came over them. They had not known that such could happen so quickly. But now it was there. They stormed away and closed ranks and became a mob. They were accompanied by the invisible being that the cry of murder had called forth. It ran with them.

'Catch him!'

'Get the word around!'

They had never believed that anything could spread like this from man to man, like fire in straw. But now it did. They appeared from all sides. People from the island, all of them. Now they rose up, like a nameless, raging pack.

Into the woods where the man had disappeared. There they ran into something tall and dark. Kari Ness. Just standing there erect and unmoving.

They did not hear what she said.

13

Andreas West!

He thought he heard the calling again. But not like a friendly calling in front of him now, but like the half-choked baying of a hound behind him. His shattered nerves throbbed and surged inside him. Fear had gripped him at the moment the crime was committed. Flashes of light shot up and illuminated all the ugly memories – then a dim twilight settled down over them again.

He ran desperately. The mob was at his heels. The meaningless call sounded behind him:

Andreas!

Who knows my name here?

No, no name was called. He ran on.

His pursuers rushed around aimlessly. They had no other glimpse of their prey than the one they got when they ran into him at the scene of the murder. He had slipped away from them like a shadow and been cunning enough to keep to the thickest groves. But they'd flush him out sooner or later. He could not escape them on this tiny island.

The thought served to inflame them: he can't help but fall into our hands.

Then a woman screamed:

'Help! I saw him! He was ugly as the devil. Over here! Catch him!'

She screamed deliriously. The handsome stranger had been transformed before her eyes. They ran toward her without an instant's hesitation.

People appeared from everywhere and joined the mob. Familiar, peaceful people. Now they were transformed. Four men came running from the opposite direction and shouted:

'Watch the boats! Post a guard at every boat.'

Two women shouted:

'Yes, he's on an island. He can't get away!'

Suddenly a man came running from a side path – with another man at his heels. They stormed right through the middle of the mob. The murderer! With Rolf just behind him. Then Rolf stumbled over a tree root and the fleeing man escaped. Cut through their midst and disappeared. They came to life:

'That was him!'

'Where'd he go?'

Rolf jumped to his feet. His face was completely unrecognizable, distorted by sorrow and rage.

'Didn't you see him?' he shouted.

A woman waved her arms wildly:

'I saw him! He was ugly as – I've never seen anything so horrible in all my life!'

Rolf was like a flame. He set fire to those around him. They saw him and followed him. He shouted:

'Come on! Over here! This way – '

He ran at their head.

As they ran they were accompanied by something they could not see, but clearly felt. Murder itself. Sin. Disaster. Rage. – They had no name for it, only feelings. It whipped them into a wild, uncontrollable frenzy.

They had lost sight of their prey. He had sunk into the earth again. But they'd find him!

'Spread the word!'

14

THE WORD SPREAD like fire around the island.

Gudrun and her husband, Ivar, were sitting at home. They were sitting together in one chair.

'Know what I did?' asked Gudrun. 'I told Inga all about it.'

'I just bet you did,' answered Ivar. 'And a lot of others, too, I can imagine.'

'Oh, no. A secret's a secret. But I'll make sure that people can see it as soon as possible. You don't understand how it is, any of this.'

'No, I guess I don't – '

'What's that?'

Ivar jumped up from the chair so quickly that Gudrun tumbled onto the floor.

'What is it?' he said.

It was one of the neighbors who had stuck his head in through the door. Stiffly, for he was accompanied by Murder.

'Quick! Inga's been killed!' he shouted.

'Catch the murderer!' he shouted again and threw the fire into the house, the wild rage that could spread and consume all.

A second of silence. Then it caught. The raging fire, not to be understood at the moment. It just caught and ·flamed up. They rushed out of their house.

Gudrun ran out and shouted:

'It's not two hours since I – no, it – it can't be – '

The neighbor said as they ran:

'And the sheriff's away. There's no one here to take charge of the hunt.'

Ivar replied, as the rage took hold of him:

'No, but he'll not get away from us.'

They rushed out onto the green fields and into the verdant groves – surrounded by the quiet sea. Far away lay other islands where nothing was known of all this.

At Lee they were struggling to get the dead sows out of the well. In the pens, the baby pigs that had lost their mothers grunted and squealed. Bergit was keeping a close watch ·over the latest born so that no more would be eaten.

The boar ran around and around grunting in his cage. He had gotten his body moving again. Was excited and vicious. He hacked at the fence a bit. No one paid any attention to it, he could not get out.

Jens and the clipper were at work at the well. Helga was helping them, as well as another man who had been called from the neighboring farm. One of them lowered himself down and tied a strong rope around the body of the sow on top. Then they all hauled, and the heavy, grey-white sow rose up, spilled over the edge of the well and fell in a heap on the grass. With a broken neck; the pit in her brow empty and cold and dark for always.

Jens was sullen, thinking about his loss. The wildness from before was gone, there was no trace of it left but two dead sows. A clear loss that he just had to accept. A loss for all his work and expense.

They hoisted the other sow up. But that was all. They heard a shout behind them as they stood there and evaluated the clear, cold truth.

One of the neighbors came on the run. He looked around shyly, up toward Karl and Mari's house, saw no one there, and said wildly:

'Come on. Help catch the murderer!'

'Murderer?' The word spread over them.

'Inga's been killed,' explained the man. 'You'll have to tell them.' He nodded toward the house.

Helga screamed and ran into the barn to her mother. Jens grew pale. Inga?

'And the murderer's still at large. Come on!'

The fire. It flamed up. They were already running. Then the neighbor stopped:

'You'll have to tell them. Are they home?'

'Just Mari's home. Karl went to town today. You tell her!'

'No!'

Bergit and Helga came running out in alarm.

'Go in and tell her,' Jens said to Bergit.

It was natural that she do it. She did not object.

The others were already running.

Bergit was left standing there alone with her responsibility.

The fire spread to every home. Where there were children, not all could follow the call. Someone had to remain at home. Women. All the men joined the chase. The larger children were hastily told not to go, but paid no attention and mixed in with the grown-ups.

It reached everyone.

At a table sat a sullen couple eating supper. The wife was waiting for a chance to begin a quarrel.

'How's the soup today?'

C

'Oh – '

'Just like I say: I'll never see the day when the food I prepare is to your liking.'

The husband crossly stirred the soup with his spoon.

'Liking and liking – ' he began, but got no farther. A man burst in, muddy, his face distorted and unrecognizable. The rage was in him. He brought the fire that flamed up.

'Come on, you two!' he shouted, without thinking to tell them why.

'What's the matter?'

'A girl's been killed. Come on!'

The woman jumped up.

'My God! Who?'

'The girl at Lee. We've got to catch him, he's still on the loose!'

The fire was in the house.

Don't think! Just race off with the mob.

Outside they heard shouting a ways off.

'Over there! Come on!' shouted the man.

They heard how he was thirsting for the life of the fleeing man. They were swept along by it. Fire from below. Listen! It flamed up in them all: the chase is on. –

15

HILL AND DALE carried Inga home. They were temporarily cut off from taking part in the chase. A man was sent to the next island to fetch the doctor, even though there was nothing that could be done.

They walked along, bearing a hastily made stretcher. They heard the chase rushing through the woods around them. They felt a prickling in their bodies, an urge to take part. They were no longer drunk. The situation had totally and strangely altered their faces.

When the shouts grew sharper they set the stretcher down and said:

'Now they've got him.'

'Oh, no, not yet,' they decided, picked up the stretcher again and walked along rapidly. Toward Lee.

The beer had left only a heaviness in their limbs. They clutched the stretcher in their huge hands. They carried the light girl as if she were a feather.

They did not look forward to arriving. They set the stretcher down in a grove and Dale entered the yard to see if he could find someone. Two dead sows lay beside the well by the barn. That was strange.

He found Bergit at home, sitting stiffly and erectly in a chair. He saw that she knew all about it.

'We've got her outside.'

'Well, take her in. Mari's in there alone.'

'Does she know about it?'

Bergit nodded.

'Yes, she knows now – I was in there.'

'That's good.'

He wanted to leave, but could not hold back a question:

'What happened to those sows?'

'Oh, them – ' she answered evasively.

Dale felt ashamed at having asked, and returned to Hill waiting in the grove.

They picked up the stretcher and carried it in.

Mari Lee saw them coming and met them in the yard. She was calm. Bergit had prepared her.

'Where's Rolf?' she asked.

'He's chasing the man,' they answered, and felt the urge within themselves to join the mob.

'We'd better join them now,' they said. 'Where'll we put her?'

She showed them the way to a pale, adolescent, feminine room on the second floor of the house. It was strange there. They walked softly and thought, without fully understanding: this is how Inga wanted her room to be.

'We'd better hurry and join them,' they said and carried the rough stretcher out with them again.

They listened. A wild chase over there. They ran toward it. To free themselves. Free themselves.

16

IT WAS ABOUT TIME for Karl Lee to come home. He always came home at a set time from these trips to town.

Mari Lee stood in the yard listening. Rolf had not come home yet. She heard shouts and cries down in the woods. Only she and Bergit were home at Lee. Helga had also run off. Bergit had fled to her own house after having delivered the message.

A motor puttered out at sea. Karl must be coming. Mari Lee walked down to the small pier. On the way she heard how the chase raged through the groves and gullies nearby. What sort of man was it who could keep hidden away so long? He must have possessed the wiliness of an animal.

It would be difficult to say what Mari Lee was thinking as she walked along. Her thoughts still moved heavily. It was the first gasping silence after the blow.

Lost, she thought dully. It's lost.

You mold and turn them and watch over them. Thousands and thousands of turnings – and then they're gone just as soon as they're ready.

There, he's landing now. He knows nothing of it yet. He has little time left to feel safe and calm. Now for once he too will be knocked off balance.

Inga is dead.

Her thoughts came in starts. Then they stopped, to collect themselves.

Look, there's another man with him. They're laughing. Karl's laughing. I'll put a stop to that. Oh, help me, God; have we drifted so far apart that I can have such thoughts?

I need him now. His calm strength. I mustn't lose him.

Lose him? Who's talking about that? No one, she thought, but I still mustn't lose him.

They stepped onto the rickety pier. The other man walked off in a different direction. Karl Lee came up the hill.

He started when he saw his wife waiting for him. He could see that something was wrong.

'What's the matter?'

She found that she could not just blurt it out as she had planned. She said:

'Prepare yourself, Karl.'

He stiffened. She thought about how wild guesses were racing through his mind, how in all haste room was being cleared in there to receive the coming sorrow. Enough room so that it could hold it safely.

Now you're being considerate, she thought about herself.

'Tell me, then.'

She told him. Saw how he took it. He had cleared enough room so that he could stand there and give the message lodgings far inside him.

They stood there together in silence.

The chase suddenly came toward them, wild and tumultuous. A wing of the mob passed close by.

'They're chasing him,' she said, hesitant, almost ashamed of the wild cries these peaceful people now were using.

Karl Lee shook himself. It was all so ugly and unrecognizable and foreign to the spirit he had built up in his home. He listened to the blood-thirsty shouts of the mob:

'There he goes!'

'This way!'

'Where?'

Then a vicious command:

'After him, God damn it all –!'

Karl Lee jumped. The commanding voice was that of his son, Rolf. He ran past in a frenzy, shouting and cursing.

'Where's Rolf?' Karl Lee asked, unbelieving.

She had not recognized her son's voice, but answered, frightened: 'He's with them.'

'They're beside themselves,' she added.

Three men burst out of the bushes. Friends of theirs, but beside themselves because murder was still running with them, stirring up the wildness buried deep down inside them. They did not even recognize the two parents, just shouted:

'He was just here! Watch that boat! He's in that grove over there!'

Karl Lee was touched by the flame in the shout and started running without thinking.

His wife grabbed his arm.

'Where are you going? Don't go with them. Come home with me.'

He grew calmer.

'All right,' was all he said, and bowed his head.

They remained standing there a moment. They'd better go home.

The chase went in the direction of the grove. The pursuers stormed in that direction. But they were on the wrong track again. He was right there after all. He burst out of the bushes and ran close by the two parents. He sensed that they would not run after him, stopped and pleaded, out of breath:

'Help me.'

His eyes wavered and shone. Something had been extinguished behind them. They were not the eyes of a man in full control of himself, but of one ruined by life.

Karl Lee asked:

'Who are you?'

His wife cried out:

'It's him!'

The man was off like a shot. He ran with unbelievably long strides.

Mari Lee repeated:

'That was him!'

'Yes, I could see that. And also that he wasn't sane.'

Not sane. – Though it was perhaps foolish, they felt relieved at the thought. She had been killed by someone out of his mind. That wasn't quite so horrible.

The bushes rustled again. Rolf burst out.

'Over here!' he shouted over his shoulder as he caught a glimpse of his prey.

Karl Lee called to him:

'Rolf! Stop!'

Rolf did not hear. He was like a dog on the scent. He disappeared.

His parents were left standing there, stiff, silent. They'd better go home. Inga lay there. They had to face the truth.

Mari Lee said finally:

'Was this also the will of God?'

Her husband heard something close to an accusation in her tone of voice. There was no reason for it, but she said it that way. He answered coldly and evasively:

'How should I know?'

They went home.

17

THE FIRE SPREAD FROM ROLF. He was the spark, inflaming the others just by the way he ran. Blindly. Relentlessly, his face transformed.

Sometimes he led, sometimes joined the mob. They watched him and were swept along – both because he looked like he did and because he was the brother of the murdered girl. But mostly because he was so transformed. It reverberated deep inside them. Something in them cried out for gratification: a need to express vile and foul impulses.

Catch the murderer and turn him over to the police? That wasn't enough. That would not conciliate that which had stepped out of the shadows of their souls. It could not so easily be satisfied and calmed.

No. Only a life could still this need.

A desperate man was fleeing from them. Catch him –

The more they ran, the less they reasoned why they longed for blood. But they longed for the blood of their prey. And they would soon get it. He could not escape them. They watched Rolf as they ran, opened themselves to him to be infected. Shouted and screamed. Rolf ran in silence. They were all headed for the deep pit within themselves, led by Rolf.

What was going on inside Rolf? He was beyond that stage. Nothing was going on inside him. Just inner turmoil. He had seen his sister lying there. Among tall, blossomless plants. Everything had stopped. He had stood face to face with the murderer. He had seen his crazed eyes for a second. At that instant the fire was lit. Sorrow was converted into rage, into killing lightning that did not strike down from the heavens, but that ran along the ground, consuming all before it, blinding all reason. He was lost, he who fled before them.

Children also ran with the mob. Boys with bulging eyes.

'Hooray!' they shouted. 'You'll never catch him!'

'Just give up!'

'He's too fast for you!'

Parents stumbled upon their children. They suddenly saw their own flesh and blood before them. From the depths of their derangement, from the depths of their own humiliation they saw their children, were shocked, and wanted to turn back. My own child –

Then they became aware of the shouts and reached for accustomed and worn-out words of rebuke:

'Just stop that now! How dare you? Be quiet! Mind your tongue!'
– Words that come as from a machine as soon as children step out
of line. Then the rage swept over them again and they were once
more caught up by it. Engulfed. Filled with thoughts of murder.
This could not be stopped. Rolf ran in and out of the mob like
a shuttle.

At the outer edge appeared a tall, dark figure now and then and
waved long arms in their direction: Kari Ness. No one paid any
attention to her.

18

No farm on the island was so poor that it did not have an orchard.
The trees stood in rows on sun-glutted south slopes, backed by the
buildings of the farm, covered now with half-ripened fruit, bowed
low in rain and sunshine. Paradise.

And most of all in the orchard at Lee. With the huge red barn
behind it.

The chase now stormed in that direction. The murderer was
driven toward Lee, where his victim lay. He had been driven out
of all the hiding-places he had found and was out in the open. He
had to flee somewhere. He raced toward the orchard he saw before
him.

In back of it the sun shone directly down on the dark red wall of
the barn, and gave it the appearance of a sacrificial altar in the midst
of all that fruitfulness. Warm, still, dark, red. And with the breath
of the sea over it.

They thought, in their confused minds:

Crush him against the wall.

Someone said out loud:

'He's headed for the barn. We've got him trapped!'

The terrain was such that their prey had only one choice: into
the orchard.

He was ringed in on all sides. His pursuers had organized themselves in the open fields.

They could not see him, but knew he was in the orchard. They closed in.

There were hundreds of trees in the orchard, and row upon row of berry bushes that afforded cover. But he was trapped there and the mob knew it would soon have him.

They spread out. Rolf came on the run. Gudrun was at his heels. She had been running wildly with the mob the whole time. Now she suddenly threw herself to the ground:

'I can't go any farther! I don't want to, either.'

Rolf shouted at her:

'What's the matter with you? Get up!'

She looked at him and suddenly saw him as he now was: transformed by evil. She was repulsed by all that was a part of him.

'Get away from me!' she cried out, and suddenly felt ill. 'Get away from me! I can't go on. And I don't want to, either.'

Rolf had not waited to listen to her. He no longer cared about her, but set off at a run between the rows of trees of the orchard. Between the trees, and the rows of raspberry and currant bushes. He heard shouts at a distance. They must have caught sight of something.

'There he goes!' came a shout.

Gudrun still lay on the ground. Exhausted. She tried to get a grip on herself and become a human being again.

'Inga,' she said softly, without reason or meaning. She started at the sound of her own voice.

The bushes beside her rustled. A handsome man burst out of them and threw himself down in front of her. She screamed when she saw who it was. He was on the point of collapsing. And his eyes shone with a light she had never seen before. He fastened them on her:

'Help me,' he pleaded. Breathless.

He was spent.

'Hide me! They're after me.'

Gudrun tried to push the sight away. She was beside herself with fear.

'Go away! I haven't done you any harm,' she shouted at him.

His head flopped weakly from side to side.

'Harm?' he repeated in confusion. 'Just hide me somewhere.'

But Gudrun had thoughts only for her own plight.

'I'm going to have a baby. I don't want to die!' she cried.

'Die?' the man replied. 'I don't want to die, either.'

Gudrun looked at him in alarm, but then realized that it was not she who was in danger. She saw how doomed he was, he who lay before her.

'No one can help you,' she said bluntly.

'They're after me. They'll tear me to pieces!' the crazed man said. 'Tear me to pieces. I'm afraid. Help me!'

Gudrun wanted to say something more to him, but could not. She had stood up and was standing under a tree. She said again, almost tonelessly:

'No one can help you.'

She did not understand the rigid, glistening set of his face, the streams of sweat and the hair plastered down over his face. He was at one and the same time distracted and terrified by things to come. He lay on the ground at her feet and gathered strength for a new flight. She saw how much he needed to lie there and rest his legs. She was also tired and hot and confused, but he was much worse off. He was to be destroyed – the mob at his heels left no doubt of that. No one could help him. She did not understand how she could say such hard words to him, but she had said them. They struck him like blows. Heavy blows against his failing nerves.

He was not handsome now.

She wanted to say something to make up for what she had already said. But what was the use of it? She understood that he was no longer in full possession of his senses. This realization made her feel sorry for him. His crime no longer seemed so black.

The mob was upon them, just on the other side of the bushes. Loud cries reached their ears.

The man at her feet jumped up. He had gathered the strength he needed. He said something to her, quickly, something of what was churning around inside his brain:

'I don't want to die. I can't die. Tell them that!'

Then he fled and was quickly out of sight. She collected herself and turned toward the charging mob, ready to deliver his message to them.

And I'm going to have a baby, she thought impulsively.

The first person she saw was her husband, Ivar. They had been separated during the chase. Now he was leading the pack. But was that Ivar? She called to him as soon as she saw him:

'Ivar!'

But he ran past, on among the trees. Gone. And I'm bearing his child, she thought in despair. She had no strength left to continue.

The whole mob rushed past. With Rolf at its heart. It was horrible to see them. Gudrun wanted to tell them that the man who had committed the crime was not in his right mind. That would soften them, she thought.

They tossed shouts and questions at her:

'Where'd he go?'

'He said – ' she began and tried to deliver the message from him. They did not stop to listen to her. Someone shouted:

'There he goes – !'

He had appeared for a second between the trees. He was trapped and headed for the sun-filled spot beneath the red wall of the barn.

They rushed off after him. Gudrun called after them that he was afraid to die. They heard it no more than if she had never said it.

Gudrun's knees gave way. She sank down. The hard words she had said to the fleeing man tormented her.

The chase was entering its final stage in the fertile orchard. The man was driven into an ever-narrowing wedge.

'We've got him!'

They did not have their hands on him yet, but they soon would. He ran out of the last hiding-place and straight into a red wall. A huge wall, it seemed to him. His brain pounded. He no longer heard a voice calling Andreas West! like heavenly bells, only a pounding and throbbing. The air stood still. The sun baked down on the spot in front of the wall where he stood facing his pursuers.

'There he is!'

They stormed toward him. Behind them a voice called out:

'Stop!'

Several of the mob turned and looked. Karl Lee came running up. It was he who had called out. But most of them no longer responded to shouts and orders; they had been shouting and screaming too much themselves.

There stood the guilty man, and they were over him in a flash. He stood as if nailed to the red wall. The flames blazed up fiercely in them now that they had their victim before them. They threw themselves over him like a pack of dogs, with Rolf in the middle. Even he had not heard his father's command. Karl Lee was nearer now and his voice was harsher:

'Stop that, I say!'

It was useless. Deep inside the human consciousness dwell grating, throaty, bestial sounds that now rose up and drowned out all others.

No sound came from the hunted man. This was his judgement. His expiation. He was sacrificed before the towering red wall and his blood trickled down toward the roots of the fruit trees in the orchard below.

The orchard was rich with fruit – but narrow, hot, too confining to breathe in.

Karl Lee had reached them, and forced his way through the crowd to his son.

'Rolf, what do you think you're doing ?!'

Rolf was still wild:

'Let me go, you – '

He saw who it was, and suddenly grew silent. The igniting flame flickered and went out.

His father looked at his hands:

'Look at your hands, Rolf. Can it be possible ?'

Rolf looked at them. He started to hide them in his pockets, but stopped and let them hang at his sides.

Karl Lee called out to all of them:

'Stop now, all of you! He wasn't in his right mind!'

Rolf said:

'It's too late.'

The mob stood still. Their rage had drained out of them. They awoke from their madness and understood nothing. Look, there's Kari Ness again. At the edge of the orchard. What does *she* want here ? they thought.

There was no room to breathe beneath that stifling wall, in that air enriched by the aroma of thousands of ripening apples. That was no help. The crowd around the dead man thinned out and in its place stood a number of pitiful individuals. Wasn't he in his right mind ? That made a big difference. That made them return to their senses even faster. No, he couldn't have been in his right mind.

Rolf burst out:

'Dad!'

It was a groping cry for help, thrown out into the heavy air. The mob stood still, and woke up. Each man stood there with his heavy burden weighing on him. More people came up, those who had been too slow. The fire died down in them as soon as they arrived. The word spread like lightning: the man was crazy.

'Dad,' said Rolf again.

Karl Lee turned toward the mob, drew himself up as tall as he could, and said:

'Go now, all of you.'

Some of them stared dully at him. Some muttered under their breaths. Scraps of wildness still sat in them and could not tolerate the firmness in his voice.

It was unnecessary for him to say: human beings don't act like that! – they felt it all too well within themselves.

Rolf shook himself. But it was nothing that could be shaken off. It would not leave him. He felt as if something would relentlessly follow him, stalking along behind his back, for the rest of his life. Murder took its place there. His father seemed to notice it, for he looked shyly at Rolf.

The mob was still standing there. Then it began to break up. Away, away from that spot. They looked as if they wanted to be alone with themselves. Children were hastily pulled away. Too late. The sight was sown in them.

Two men turned and drifted back to take charge of the dead. Hill and Dale this time, too.

'What'll we do with him?' they softly asked Karl Lee.

'I don't know,' he answered without looking at them.

They turned away, and as he just remained standing there and his full weight sank down on Rolf they slowly picked up the dead man and carried him into the shade of the nearest apple tree. They sat down beside him.

'Wait there,' Karl Lee said to them. 'Come along,' he said to Rolf and pulled him away. Away from that spot.

Part 2: The Seed in the Dust

1

SOMETHING MOVES at the bottom of the pit. Mangled. Crawling.

Oppressive silence. Wakening voices deep down inside one's soul.

Take care, they say.

Who are you? they seem to ask.

You try to move, and begin lying to yourself: I had no idea. That's never happened to me before.

The voices answer: you know you're lying. The pit is in your brow.

You look at yourself, and see within yourself a sweeping landscape with vast plains and wooded mountain slopes capped with flying clouds. But you also see treacherous hidden pits, to be skirted and avoided. There are unknown things concealed in their depths. Let them lie there. No one shall know about them.

Let them lie at the bottom of the sea.

A voice breaks through:

There'll come a day when all that –

No, never! you answer hastily, desperately. But that insistent voice cannot be stilled:

There'll come a day when the sea within you shall give forth all that lies hidden in it now. Your own tiny, deep, ugly sea. Its bottom is turbulent and slimy and murky. Watch yourself!

You shove it away angrily and answer boldly: I'm not afraid.

You never figure on the slide, the avalanche that can sweep all before it and expose the landscape as it really has been all along.

Now they were fleeing.

Homeward. Or rather, simply away. The burden that weighed down on them made all their movements slow and heavy, almost deliberate. It was no wild and disordered flight. In wildness they had entered the orchard; in fear they now retired, weary and despairing, their faces turned downward.

They looked at themselves and asked:

Who are you?

And answered defiantly:

I never knew I was like that.

They remembered and shuddered: I stood over him and struck him.

Yes, but he was probably already dead then. It was Rolf who stabbed him, everyone saw that. Then I hit him. I somehow had to, though I don't know why.

Dark thoughts come drifting: I'll never have any peace of mind now. Have I disgraced myself?

Not all of them took it like that. People are different. Some of them managed to make themselves hard and say:

'Well, he had it coming, as far as I'm concerned.'

'Sure he did,' others found doubting courage to add.

There was an awkward pause and then someone tormented by his actions spoke out:

'But he wasn't in his right mind.'

'Who can be sure of that?' replied the first.

But he received little support. Most of them felt the burden weighing on them. They could not fully believe in those bold words of self-justification and would not have them for their own.

They felt, nevertheless, that they had to defend themselves. Before they knew it they were looking for a scapegoat. It was not hard to find one. Let's just get it settled right away.

Two neighbors passed each other, their heads bowed. They wanted to slip by unnoticed but one had to ask, his voice filled with horror and his eyes still on the ground:

'Can you understand that Rolf could do a thing like that?'

Don't look at him! Just answer in relief and gratitude:

'No. I wouldn't have believed it.'

Don't look at each other!

Then they were gone around the bends and behind the trees on their fertile, green island. Away from the sacrificial altar.

Gudrun walked along close behind her husband. She looked at his burdened back. For some reason they could not walk side by side. Ivar was silent.

How much was he a part of it? she thought. My baby, she thought again. Will it do anything to my baby? There were women there too, she thought in horror. If I weren't carrying my baby I'd probably have struck at him too. Look at Ivar's back. Look at him whose job it is to teach the island's children. Ivar was there and struck at the poor, crazed man.

She started. A girl came up along beside her. It was Else. A troubled and frightened girl. Rolf! Gudrun thought suddenly. She could not remember having seen Else there.

'Gudrun,' said Else.

'Yes?'

Don't look at her!

'Were you there?'

'No!' said Gudrun. But she thought to herself: yes, I was there, I was just hindered at the last moment.

Else pleaded:

'Did you see what happened?'

She didn't see it herself, thought Gudrun.

'No. I just saw them all piled up on him. That's all I saw. I just couldn't watch it.'

Else said: 'When I got there they were still all piled up. They wouldn't tell me anything. No one would tell me what happened, Gudrun.'

Gudrun did not answer. Else pleaded:

'Gudrun, what did Rolf do?'

'I don't know.'

'Do you know if he's at home? I didn't dare go in and ask when I was there. I had to find out a little something about it first.'

'Yes, he must have gone home with his father.'

They stood and waited. Each waited for the other.

'Go back there, then!' Gudrun said finally in desperation, and regretted the words immediately.

Else forgot herself and asked right out:

'Was it Rolf who did it? I saw him in the pile.'

'Wouldn't it be best for you to ask *him* that?'

Else stiffened, and realized that she had gone too far. Gudrun continued:

'I didn't see it. The men were all in a pile.'

Why did I say only the men? There were women there too.

They had slowed down, so that Ivar was far ahead of them. They saw his back. They saw him stop and let them catch up. He had heard just the same and now turned toward them. They could see that he was worse off than they were. He was ready to do disgraceful things to gain relief.

He turned to Gudrun:

'Did you say 'the men'?' he asked coldly. 'Were there only men there?'

He asked viciously, concerned only with freeing himself. There was not a speck of love for her in either his expression or in his harsh tone of voice. He was alone.

She felt ashamed of him. Because Else was a witness to this. And it chilled her to see that his love for her seemed to have disappeared.

But he had to debase himself still more in an attempt to rid himself of the responsibility. Coarsely and shamefully. He looked at Else.

'Was it Rolf you wanted to know about?' he asked.

'No!' she answered quickly. She shrank back before this coarseness that she had never seen in Ivar before. She wanted to hear nothing from this man.

But her no did not stop him. He told her:

'It *was* Rolf who did it. You were right.'

Else could not move. Blinded. Overcome. I knew it. I knew it all the time.

Gudrun was looking off in another direction.

They felt Ivar turn his back on them again. He walked off. Gudrun followed after him. Else drifted away from them.

2

HILL AND DALE were still sitting under the apple tree. They too had wanted to flee, but had turned back.

The wildness had been in them, too, and had drained out of them. Their hands had been in contact with him who lay there at their feet. They had struck that body. Their hands still bore an unpleasant memory of how the flesh gave way before the blows.

That had been the peak of senseless vengeance, followed by collapse and regret.

They had started to join the flight from the scene of the murder, but they had just a short while before carried another body. That stopped them.

Someone passing saw that they hesitated and said to them hastily, almost as a command:

'You two can see to him.'

Why us? But the man who had spoken to them was already many steps away. A respected man on the island, he as all the others.

Then they felt it: a compulsion to turn back. It grew to an urgent need. They drifted back to the spot under the towering wall.

Only Karl Lee and Rolf were still there. Then they walked off. Hill and Dale were left alone with the unknown dead man.

They looked stealthily for the places on his body where their own blows had struck him.

Dale covered him with his jacket.

What should they do with him? Where should they take him? They sat down. Tried to think about other things. Then it occurred to Hill that they should fetch the stretcher they had used once before that day. They had set it in the wood shed.

'Sure; go get it,' said Dale.

Hill walked around the barn and into the barnyard. There he met Jens who was struggling with the two sows to get them out of sight. He dragged them into a corner of the barn. All thoughts of using them in any way seemed to be gone. He looked as if he could not stand the sight of them. Hill remembered having seen Jens in the middle of the pile on top of the dead man.

'I was just going to fetch that stretcher,' he said.

Jens nodded.

'Is Karl up at the house?' Hill asked.

'Suppose so. Go up and find out.'

Jens wanted to get away. Began pulling at a sow again. Shyly, almost resentfully because Hill saw him. Get them out of sight. Don't have anything more to do with them. The memories in his hands made it impossible.

Hill did not go up to the house. He walked back around the barn with the stretcher. He and Dale laid the burden on it.

'What'll we do with him now?'

'Well, there's the barn,' said Dale.

But could they go and demand to put him there? They tried to decide if they would have allowed it if they had been in Karl Lee's position. They looked a bit indecisively at each other and said that they would. They were not quite sure if that was true.

They picked up the stretcher and walked around the corner of the barn again. The barnyard was empty now. Tiny squeals and grunts came from the pig pens.

They knocked at Karl Lee's door. No one was downstairs. Finally he came. His face was unchanged.

They pointed at the stretcher and said that it would be best to set it in the barn.

They saw that the thought repelled him. But they had said it so decidedly that there was nothing he could do.

'I suppose so,' he said.

'Maybe one of us'll sit there until it can be taken care of.'

'All right,' said Karl Lee.

He closed the door. The farm was as deserted. Hill and Dale thought that it was little help that it was the best farm on the island, with the largest and finest orchard and good buildings with thick walls and tight doors. – What help was all that? Despair crept in just as easily.

They picked up the stretcher and carried it up the ramp to the mow. The double doors stood wide open to receive the harvest. They swung on heavy hinges. Those hinges alone witnessed to the proud plans Karl Lee had had when he was young.

They tramped in.

'Smell that.'

'Yep, there's good hay in here.'

It lay there in heaps. These two men had worked at mowing and raking and pitching hay all their lives.

They set the stretcher down on two empty crates that stood there.

'There,' they said. They looked at each other.

'You can go now,' said Dale. 'I'll sit here a while.'

'No, I'll sit here,' said Hill.

They closed the double doors from the inside and sat down, both of them. They were used to being together in everything they did.

They felt old and tired. Their arms hung heavily at their sides. On the empty crates lay the burden they bore no matter how often they set it down.

They felt a need to be there. They tried to look at it as something they did that no one else would have done, and were happy when they succeeded.

They thought about her whom they had carried earlier that day. She had been as light as a feather. This burden was so heavy that they almost expected it to go crashing through the floor of the mow.

'One of us might as well go home now,' said Hill.

'Yep,' said Dale.

Neither moved. They leaned back against the wall. The low evening sun sliced through the many small cracks in the wall. The mow still held the heat of the day. The two men who sat there shivered.

They did not know how long their vigil was to last. At least all that night. In the depths of their souls they hoped that it would grant them a little absolution for their sin. But they did not tell each other that. There were perhaps many people who envied them.

Now that it was over they thought they could feel each blow they had struck. Crushing blows with heavy fists. They had had nothing sharp at hand, but probably would have used it if they had.

Doesn't it help for me to sit here?

3

KARL LEE HAD TAKEN his son home. Rolf did not go willingly. At first he had turned back and started off through the orchard, but his father ran after him and stopped him. Rolf was so exhausted that his father had no trouble catching him. They went through the orchard and along another road back to the house.

'I don't want to go home,' Rolf said, angry and confused.

'Come along now,' his father replied. His face was so rigid and stiff when he turned it toward Rolf that Rolf felt it as a compelling force.

Every time Karl Lee looked at Rolf he thought he saw something else there. Something following him. Rolf felt it so intensely that his father almost saw it. There was something about Rolf that made everyone who saw him recoil in horror.

It was hard to get him home. There were still a lot of people wandering around near the farm. People who were on the way home, but who were not quite sure if they dared. When they ran into Karl Lee and Rolf they suddenly found they were in a hurry, greeted them hastily, meaninglessly, and hurried past without looking up. They shared the burden of guilt.

Rolf repeated:

'But I don't want to go home.'

'Where else are you thinking of going, then ?'

Rolf just walked along shuffling his feet as if he could no longer lift them. That was something new for him and was part of the effect of that which followed him and weighed on him. His father thought it better to say something than to shuffle along in silence, so he continued:

'When things have gone really bad home's the only place to go. The walls of home are your only refuge.'

'No! The only thing to do then is to run away. That's what people do. You know that.'

'Yes, but it's no use. If things have gone really bad it doesn't help to fly off into something unknown. Home's the only place then.'

'So that those at home will be miserable too ?'

'Yes, those at home have to carry their share. I'll say it again: only the walls of home can shield you. Sin and sorrow and shame and everything – the home should take it all in and keep it. A home doesn't become poorer because of *that*.'

Rolf said:

'But I can see that you can hardly stand the sight of me, Dad. Not even you. What will it be like for the others then – for Mother ?'

'Do you want to run away and never see her again ?'

'Yes.'

'Well, you just come along now,' was all his father replied. 'Say, Rolf, do you have to shuffle along like that ? That's not your way of walking and you can't walk in to meet her like that.'

Someone passed them. Shyly. Furtively. Somehow defiantly. Karl Lee burst out:

'Wait a minute – '

They didn't stop to listen, just kept on walking. Kari Ness was standing at the side of the road. Was she everywhere ?

'We ought to talk together!' called Karl Lee after them.

They shut their ears to it and walked ahead as if they were afraid of being given a burden even greater than that they already bore.

'It involves my family, so we ought to be able to talk together about it,' he shouted after them. 'After we've all had a chance to think about it a bit!'

He called out in despair. He could not understand how it all would end. What he would say. But a feeling of indebtedness toward them swept over him. His children stood at the center of it all. It had all happened because Inga was dead. He felt in debt to these despairing men and women at the same time that he was shocked by their behavior.

He walked along almost numbly. It had all come upon him so suddenly that it had had an anesthetizing effect. As yet he was only shocked by what had happened.

Rolf felt it in about the same way.

'Dad!' he started to say, but came no farther.

'What do you want ?'

'Can you understand it ? Understand me ?'

His father did not answer his question, but only told him to come along.

Rolf said, frightened:

'Dad, can't you understand me?'

'I have to have a chance to think. Don't press me. Let's pull ourselves together now and go in.'

'I can't.'

'No, no; but you have to. It's up to us, your family, to help you now.'

They walked over the bright green fields of their own farm. The setting sun sent slanting rays down to the lush pastures where horses and cows were grazing. It was a good island.

They had crossed the yard and were approaching the house. Rolf stopped. His father said:

'Pull yourself together now, I said.'

'Help me, Dad. Stand on my side if anything happens.'

His father did not answer.

'Won't you?'

'I'll answer that as soon as I can. But now we'll go in. You *must*.'

4

MARI LEE COULD HEAR the tumult outside. The chase was headed for Lee.

She walked over to the window and looked out, but could see nothing. The tumult drew nearer. They must be down below the barn. She was on the point of running out, but caught herself. She attempted to shut out all the sounds and sat hunched over and trembling in a chair. Where was Rolf? Was he with them? Where was Karl? He was somewhere outside, too. Then the wild shouting died down. Thank God they had left.

Mari Lee sat alone in Inga's simple room. Inga's body was covered. Her mother thought through her whole life up to that day.

And what came of it all? she asked herself. Of all the endless preparing and thinking for the future. Now she's lying there and there's nothing more.

'Now she's lying here!' she said out loud, pronouncing the words ominously in her need. She felt it as a relief to speak out and threaten something she could not see.

She thought about it. Tried to comprehend it. She jumped when a hasty knock came at the door.

'Come in,' she called out.

It was Helga, Jens' young daughter, who came bursting in, so filled with the tidings she bore that it did not occur to her how such a room should be entered.

'Now they've killed him!' she said before she had even closed the door behind her.

'Killed? Who? Oh, no, they mustn't – '

Helga continued excitedly:

'They killed him down in the orchard. Finally they got him cornered and caught him. And then they killed him. It was awful –'

Mari Lee had jumped up. Now she sank down again.

'How did it happen?' she asked. 'Who was it – '

She stopped. Helga rattled on:

'They were all on him at once. It was terrible.'

'Oh – ' was all Mari Lee said.

She looked sharply at Helga, to see if she knew more than she had told. It did not show on her.

'Where were you when it happened?'

'I – I ran with them a while,' Helga stammered out.

Helga was also one of those who had lost Inga that day. They had grown up together from the time they were small. It had been a hard blow for Helga, too. And she had been swept along by the rage, even though she had not followed all the way. She had not completely lost her senses. She began again:

'Oh, it was terrible to see – '

Mari Lee grew impatient:

'Did you really have to take part in it?' she asked sharply.

'No, but – '

Helga felt ashamed, and turned to leave. She met Karl Lee at the door. And behind him came Rolf. She let out a soft scream of fright when she saw them.

'He's coming,' she said.

Mari Lee stood up quickly.

'What is it ?'

Helga just pushed past them and out the door, concerned only with getting away from there as quickly as possible. She closed the door after her. Karl Lee and Rolf stood just inside the room, powerless to step closer or say anything.

Mari Lee walked toward them.

'At last you've come. Did you see it ?' she asked. She started at the sight of Rolf.

'Karl, what's wrong ?'

He stood still, erect and stiff and expressionless.

'We've come home,' was all he said.

Rolf did not make a sound.

She hardly dared look at Rolf, and her voice lost its ring. He was so strange.

'It's better to tell me right out,' she said when they did not answer her immediately.

Her husband took a deep breath.

'Well, he was finally caught and killed.'

'Killed ?' she repeated. 'Yes, I've heard that. Helga told me. But who – ? Rolf, how could this happen ?'

She had sensed who bore the guilt. Rolf stood there weighed down by his burden. It was easy to see that his mother realized what was crushing him.

Karl Lee bore his share of the burden. He answered for Rolf, who could not.

'Powerful forces were released,' he said. 'That's all I can tell you.'

Mari Lee gathered strength to lift her head and look at her son.

'Come over here, Rolf. Don't just stand like that by the door. This is your home, you know.'

Rolf took a few steps forward.

'I can see you were with them.'

'Yes,' said Rolf.

'I can see more than that. Was it really you who – '

He interrupted her to say it himself:

'Yes! I did it.'

He drew strength from his defiance to continue:

'Of course I did it! I had to!'

His father said:

'It's only fair to say that they were all in on it. They were all piled up on him when I got there. I never dreamed there could be such wildness on this island.'

His wife said:

'It was all of them, then.'

'Yes, yes, but I know it was me who killed him!' Rolf said desperately. 'And everyone who was there knows it. There's no use trying to hide that, Dad.'

Karl Lee answered:

'As far as I could see, it was just that you got there first. Any one of them could have done it. But you were first.'

The others said nothing. Karl Lee spoke laboriously, but managed to continue:

'They all went away feeling guilty. They didn't try to hide how they felt.'

His wife looked at Rolf, almost without listening to what was being said. Looked shyly at Rolf.

'How could you do it, Rolf?'

'All that matters now,' said Rolf, 'is that you two can understand me. Of course, I'll be punished and all that, but that's not important. But it *is* important that you try to understand how I could do it.'

'Yes, but – ' his mother began.

Karl Lee interrupted, his voice high and troubled.

'Stop now. You have no right.'

She stopped speaking and took a step back.

'We have no right to try to understand such things. So just stop that. We have no right, Rolf.'

Mari Lee heard the hardness in his voice, so unusual for him. It meant that he could not be swayed. No right. No, they probably had no right to try to understand. She felt that was correct, but this involved Rolf and that made it somehow different. There were so many things that made you feel you could almost understand. –

Rolf had turned toward his father.

'Dad!'

'No, we have no right,' his father repeated, laboriously as before. 'Such behavior can't be understood. Or tolerated.'

Rolf began trembling.

'There's a lot at stake for me now, Dad.'

'Yes, I know it. But when you ask me to condone what you've done, I have no choice but to answer that I can't.'

Rolf saw how his father's eyes wavered indecisively while his mouth spoke such relentless words. It was hard for Rolf to imagine that what his father said could ever have been so important to him. But now it was. He felt that only that could save him. There lay Inga under a blanket. Everything connected with Inga was in a tumultuous uproar inside him.

'I thought that you two also felt that Inga – ' he began, but was interrupted.

'Don't mention her name,' his father said. 'Can't you feel that that's too much ?'

Yes, he felt that – the weight of her presence in the room. They were standing so that they had their backs toward her, but it helped little.

'I can see what you're thinking,' Rolf said to his mother.

They both looked at her. It had hit her hard. Deep shadows had fallen over her face. She did not dare to speak, but kept back that which rose up in her at the sight of Rolf's need.

Rolf called to her again.

Karl Lee's hard voice cut him off:

'You have no right to press her now. And it wouldn't be any help to you, either, to get it that way.'

'I know you can understand it if you try!' shouted Rolf. Then he realized where he was. It was a room that held death. Here one spoke softly.

'Yes, let's remember where we are,' his father said.

Rolf repeated softly:

'I know you can understand how it is for me, and I know that you want to help me.'

Karl Lee said:

'We can't grant you any pardon, Rolf.'

He stood clutching the back of a chair, as if it helped him to stand fast.

Mari Lee was silent. It was easy to see on her how much she wanted to shield her son, and yet it was as if she did not dare.

Karl Lee drew himself up straight and continued, his voice foreign and forced:

'For every step we took on the way home I grew more and more afraid of this. I felt clearly that I would have to say no to you, Rolf. Violence must not be tolerated.'

'But what about his violence?' said Rolf. 'Is that to be tolerated and pardoned?'

'No, but that's no excuse for your doing the same. And he wasn't in his right mind either, as far as I can understand it. I spoke to Gudrun who saw him up close. And I saw him myself. He was insane. But you and the others who were after him were sane.'

Rolf looked at his father in utter confusion. Then he asked once more if he were to be turned out.

'Turned out? Didn't you hear me tell you that your home is the only thing that can shield you?'

'But you *are* turning me out, Dad. I'm just to be thrown away.'

His father replied:

'Not at all! We want to form a shield for you. Don't try to break it down and bring on more disaster. But we have to condemn what you've done. You'll have to make up for it, Rolf. There's no other way.'

'Make up for it?'

'Yes. Within yourself. You just come and demand pardon for a murder. But you can never get it.'

'Just the same I know you can understand me.'

'I can't understand you. I thought that such wildness was beyond you.'

'Just the same I know you can understand me.'

They looked each other in the eye. Karl Lee appeared not to have so much strength left either. He heard Mari say, frightened, and as a warning:

'Be careful now – '

'Rolf, you support me in what I'm doing just the same,' Karl Lee said. 'You know very well that you do, now that you've calmed down a bit. You've learned to think well enough so that you can understand that we can't possibly accept what you've done. You're just trying to force this through, even though you know it's no use.'

'Could you have looked calmly on ? I don't think so.'

His father writhed at the question.

'No, you can't answer that,' Rolf said.

'I would have stopped myself from killing him. We ought to be able to control ourselves that much. All of those who took part are now crushed by shame and regret.'

Rolf said:

'Well, I think fate was kind to you when it arranged for you to be away. None of us believed beforehand that we would behave as we did. But those who were spared should try to understand it.'

'I just don't understand why all this happened!' Karl Lee burst out. 'Why an abyss of violence and wildness suddenly has to open up. But we have to call it what it is.'

Rolf could hold up under it no longer. He stumbled toward the door.

'Yes, yes, yes, yes,' he muttered. Weary. Defeated.

His mother looked up.

'Are you leaving ? Don't!'

Rolf did not answer. He pushed past his father. Karl Lee said:

D

'No, let him go off by himself a little, to think. Leave him alone with it a while.'

'Don't go, Rolf.'

Rolf did not stop. He walked slowly, the shadow still at his heels. He closed the door behind him.

His mother wanted to run after him, but Karl Lee stood blocking the door.

'No, Mari.'

'What have you done now ?' she asked.

'I did what I felt was my duty. But don't run after him. Leave him alone a bit.'

She looked at him resentfully.

'God help you for what you have done.'

He did not answer.

'It was terrible that you couldn't comfort him the least bit. He turned only to you.'

'Comfort him ? I couldn't give him what he wanted. That's all.'

They sat there, tormented and laid waste. Each of them saw how exhausted the other was. They started to approach each other, but stopped. Their thoughts began to relax. They sat facing the covered body of their daughter.

5

ROLF WALKED OUT of the yard. Aimlessly, hopelessly. He felt that there was someone behind him, but when he turned there was no one there. He saw only the farm.

There's the farm I should have inherited.

He looked down on the farm from the hill above. It looked especially fine from up there. A fine farm. Well, someone would work it, even if he never did. Someone had to make use of such a farm.

He walked on. Westward. The farm passed out of sight. He still felt followed. A little while later he came walking from the west and disappeared to the east. Then a little later he came from the east walking west. Each time he saw the farm where he belonged.

You're wandering around like a lunatic, he told himself. What are you always gaping at the farm for?

There was no one in sight down there.

He walked past, headed east.

I have to go see Else.

He was not too eager about it. He had lied to her and not behaved as he should have. But he was in need now. It can't be helped! She loves me, and so I have to go to her.

What a wretch you are.

Sure, I am. But she'll understand me. I need to hear that someone understands me. Anyone put in the spot I'm in would do the same thing, he thought hatefully, prompted by all that tormented him.

I'll go to Else.

He walked through the woods. There was no one on the road. The island was as deserted. Everybody had fled to his den. Each farm seemed to be walled in.

Not even Kari Ness appeared. But she would certainly come.

See, there lay the farm where Else lived. Her father and brother had taken part in the chase. Now they sat somewhere in the house and tried to ease their consciences. There was no one in the yard. But several windows were open because of the heat. The window in Else's room was one of them. Else is sitting in there and can't breathe.

Rolf took advantage of the open window. He stopped behind a bush and whistled a signal that he and Else used. It was quiet in the house. She could easily hear the signal. My sweetheart is outside whistling for me. My sweetheart is a murderer.

There she was.

He saw her face at the window. He whistled once more. The face was gone.

A little while later she came out. He stepped back among thicker bushes and gave the signal. It was like an eerie imitation of a game.

'Rolf!'

She stood before him, looking at him in confusion. He searched her features, and thought he saw love there. But most clearly he saw horror, and shock.

'What do you want?'

'Do you find it strange that I want to see you. I've got to talk to you!'

She answered, frightened:

'Can't it wait until another time?'

'No, it has to be now.'

He saw that she was afraid of him. It hurt him to see it.

'Are you going back in?'

She stopped. He saw that she was on the point of running back to the sturdy house where she had been born and raised and which was a fortress for her in moments of trouble.

She said:

'I can't talk to you right now.'

He caught and held her. A familiar arm around her, so familiar that neither of their bodies reacted against it. He felt again that she was afraid of him.

'Let me go,' she said.

'No, I'm not going to let you go.'

'But I'm afraid of you, Rolf.'

It hurt him terribly that she said it like that. She meant so much to him, even though he had lied to her. Now he could have said: you're important to me, and it would have been the truth. He asked:

'Are you really afraid of me?'

'Yes. I don't understand – '

A shock ran through him at her words. It was all precisely a matter of understanding or not.

'Don't you understand, Else? I really have to know what you think about what I've done, and if you think you *can* understand it. Or have I become a stranger to you?'

She did not answer.

'Won't you even try to understand?' he pleaded, discarding all show of pride.

She looked at him shyly, but saw only that which was following him, and was blinded by it.

'Have you become a stranger to me? No, you can never be that, but – let me go!'

'But what – ?'

Yes, he saw love in her face, but she was so frightened that she did not dare give way to it.

'Maybe 'stranger' is the right word for it after all,' she said and struggled to express what she felt. 'In a way,' she continued, 'because I really didn't know what you were capable of doing, not until today.'

'Do you know just exactly what you're capable of doing at all times, Else?'

She stammered in reply:

'N – no, but – no, I guess not.'

She was silent. Did not dare look at him. Every time she tried she found she could not.

'You look at me as if I were someone else.'

She said softly:

'You are someone else. Someone I don't know. Please believe me, Rolf, when I tell you it's hard for me to say that,' she added.

Rolf did not hear these last words. He was sunk too deep in his need. He was filled by a blind seeking for something firm to grasp and hold.

'If I hadn't done what I did,' he said, 'it would have only been because I wasn't really fond enough of Inga.'

'When you put it like that –. But it's – well, it's just not like that, and you know it, too. We learned that in school together.'

Why did she have to remind him of those days ? When they were children together.

'Please don't bring that up, Else.'

'All right.'

'We were talking about trying to understand what I've done,' he said hoarsely.

'Yes, but let's think about it a bit first, and about us. In peace.'

He repeated her words:

'Think about it. In peace. Do you think there's much time for that, for me ? It just looks to me like you're trying to get rid of me. And have nothing more to do with me. Don't you even dare look at me ?'

'Please don't force me to any decision now, Rolf. Please!'

He finally let go of her.

'There. You're free now. I can see how it is. Just go now. I'm not worth anything else!'

She didn't go. Stood still. Rolf said:

'You won't say what you really mean. But I can say it for you.'

'No, you can't!'

'And you keep thinking now that it's not so many hours since you noticed that I was tired of this between us. Tired of you. Don't try to deny it, you could see I was, and I was, too. And now – '

'That's enough now, Rolf. Let's talk about it another time.'

Else wanted to leave, but somehow could not bring herself to it. It began to get dark. It was strangely quiet. Not a breath of wind. Not a sound.

'It's getting dark,' she said.

'*You* can't understand me either.'

'Rolf, let me think about it a bit. I've got to go now.'

He said in sudden anger:

'Well, can't you see I've let go of you ?'

She jumped.

'Yes, but – '

'So you can just go whenever you want.'

'Rolf, this is terrible.'

'Yes,' he answered, and continued in a hard, sharp tone of voice that dug a ditch between them:

'If you'd really loved me, you wouldn't have let me down because of this.'

'I guess not,' she replied, hurt and bitter.

'Are you mad at me?'

'You seem to think you know everything. But I know something, too.'

'Do you really – '

'I know that there's something about you that keeps us apart. What is it that's always kept us apart when I wanted to love you? You haven't loved *me!*' she concluded loudly.

He let it pass. It made no difference now. He had worked himself into a rage. He said quickly:

'Well, I'm tired of it all – so now you know.'

'What?'

She stared at him in fear.

'So now you know it!' he replied wildly. 'So now you can go.'

She took a couple of steps backwards.

'But, Rolf – '

They both felt how something fell apart and crumbled to dust. He saw that she had loved him. She had not fully believed what she had said, but now that she saw that it was true, that which had loved him within her went its way.

He wanted to say something. Then he saw that he was left standing alone.

He also walked away.

6

IT WAS GETTING DARK.

That was usually a welcome sign for those working in the fields as evening approached in late summer. They waited for it, accepted it gratefully and walked home from the day's toil.

This evening it was different. They saw it with apprehension: the light is dying. It will be still worse now.

The twilight drifted in from the sea. And settled down on, or rose up out of, the earth. But this evening it did not come in friendliness.

The people of the island saw it come and thought only of the night that would follow in its wake.

They themselves were filled with the twilight. They could not understand it. It came from somewhere beyond the known. From treacherous pits that had opened up.

Night is coming.

They sat in their houses, stood in their yards. In their gardens and orchards and private rooms. They did nothing, they only looked up in amazement now and then and became aware of where they were: What am I doing here? What did I come here for?

Way off they could see the farm at Lee. They looked in that direction. The barn towered up before their eyes. They wished it would sink into the earth with all it contained. But it did not; such things do not sink down, but grow and increase until they are three times as large as they really are.

Two women met on the road, each carrying a milk pail since it was evening. They still had to have food and milk, and the cows still gave milk – it was all just a habit that they did not need to think about. Their eyes and thoughts were turned toward the barn at Lee.

They stopped and said it was hot. They turned unconsciously toward Lee. Looked at the farm that could be seen from almost all parts of the island. One of them said:

'Well, things'll sure be different up at Lee now.'

'Yes, it wasn't enough that – '

'Rolf – '

'Yes, that Rolf was so wild.'

'I would have thought he had learned to control himself better.'

They turned it toward Rolf as quickly as they could. Thank God there was someone to put the blame on.

'Yes, it was all Rolf's fault,' the other replied. 'He started it all.'

'Sure he did. Everyone knows that.'

'And it was he who *did* it.'

'Sure, who in the world else would ?'

'The others just followed him, that's all. But thank God they could control themselves.'

They looked questioningly at each other. How much are you ready to agree to ? There was no danger. No harm had been done.

Where were *you* ?

That was not asked. A quick glance they gave each other told them that they had seen each other by the red wall. That was nothing to talk about.

'Yes, that Rolf – '

'Well, it's no help that they go to school up there at Lee; that's easy enough to see.'

'Oh, that studying doesn't lead to anything good. They never finish it, anyway.'

'No, just look at the father.'

'And then he turned to building.'

'Yes, that sure gave people a good laugh.'

'Yes, indeed, those folks at Lee – '

'What do you think'll happen to Rolf.'

'He'll probably be punished for it.'

'Oh, sure, he'll be punished for it.'

'I just can't figure it out – I almost knew something awful would happen up at Lee some day. They don't act like other people.'

They got no farther in their self-debasement, for the gravel on the road began crunching. They started at the sound, even though it was something they heard every day.

It was Kari Ness, terrifyingly large and real. They had never seen a woman so tall and dark. They could not move. The self-defenses they had been building up fell to pieces as the twilight slowly spread its frightening web over them.

Kari Ness stepped out of the drifting dusk and said to them:

'You two might as well go on up to Lee this evening too. They're gathering there in the barn.'

She did not ask them if they wanted to.

They did not answer, either. Tried only to get a grip on themselves. What are you so afraid of? It's only Kari Ness – you know her.

But she's so terrifyingly large. –

She stood erect and threatening before them and no matter how they tried they could not reduce her to normal size. She spoke to them again:

'Didn't you hear?'

They felt her voice cut through them.

'Yes, yes,' they answered quickly.

'Well, go then. I think you probably need it.'

They heard her, as they had so often heard Kari Ness say things they had then quickly forgotten and not troubled themselves with. But now they listened to her with respect.

'Has Karl sent word?' one of them ventured to ask.

'He didn't have to,' she answered.

No. That was true. Now that they had received word they would go – no matter what it brought.

Her eyes were fastened on them. What was it about Kari Ness today? They looked down. It was good they had received word, anyway. Now there would be a place to be during the coming restless, waking night. Restless searching – but now a goal had been set. They had known it all along, but until now it had not been said. Go to the red barn. He is lying there, he who binds you.

'Are you going to spread the word around?' they asked respectfully.

Kari Ness nodded.

Then she lost some of her resolution, and said fiercely:

'Not a bird falls to the earth but that it is the will of God.'

There she stood, she whom they knew. Quick as lightning they sensed her doubt, clung to it, and asked:

'Is that what you really believe?'

She answered fiercely. Fiercely and loudly:

'God help us to believe it!'

She strode off.

The two women said nothing to each other.

To Lee, they thought. And everyone will come.

7

'IT'S GETTING DARK,' said Mari Lee.

Karl Lee answered without lifting his head:

'So I see.'

They were still sitting in Inga's room.

We'll sit in this room the rest of our days. No matter where we are, we'll always be in this room.

They could have said this to each other, but it was not necessary.

Outside the day drifted away. The day of disaster was over. The approaching night was inescapable.

Mari Lee repeated:

'It's getting dark quickly.'

'So I see.'

They lit a lamp. Then sat down again. Listened tensely. They did not hear the sound they were waiting for: steps approaching up the stairs.

Rolf did not come. His mother said:

'Are you sorry now, Karl?'

'No.'

She was not sure that he spoke with as much conviction as before. She could make him doubt still more. No! Forgive me.

'But he hasn't come back.'

'Be quiet,' he said. 'Don't say things like that.'

They sat in silence a while and listened for footsteps. Then she said:

'It was you who drove him out.'

'Yes, if you want to call it that.'

'But he's my child, too.'

He answered:

'I'm shaking like a leaf for him.'

That made her sit quietly a while as they continued to listen for something to step out of the evening outside. Nothing came. She said finally:

'He didn't get much support from you.'

'No.'

'But he had a right to demand some, since you're his father.'

'I've told you why I couldn't give him any. That's all there is to it.'

'Yes, that's all there is to it, but – '

'He's still alive!' he said.

He said it with such conviction that she wanted to take his hand. She was now standing by the window looking out. He's still alive, she thought.

She started.

'There – '

'What?'

'No, it wasn't him. People are coming.'

He stood up and looked out. Stared through the half-darkness until his eyes began to waver.

More people came.

'What does it mean?' she asked anxiously. 'Could they be bringing news of Rolf?'

'No!' he said. 'They're not walking as if they'd found something. You should be able to see that.'

They lost sight of the people. The darkness around the buildings swallowed them up.

Karl Lee thought of something:

'That's right – I said I had to talk to them.'

'When?'

'When they were on the way home before. But I don't know just what I meant by it. I shouted after them that we had to meet sometime. I somehow felt I owed it to them to say something to them. But I didn't know they'd come so soon.'

'Whatever are you going to say to them?'

'I didn't think they'd come so soon, I said.'

'I haven't sent for anyone this evening. This is something they're doing on their own,' he continued after a pause.

'Yes, but they're probably waiting for you just the same, since you asked them to come.'

They saw that more people were drifting toward the farm. Some of them were carrying lanterns, swaying lights in the growing darkness that threatened to envelop them. Jens usually hung out a lantern to light up the barnyard a bit. He came out of his house with the lantern. He was startled when the light fell on the people beside the barn. They looked as if they resented the light. Jens went back into the house.

There were people standing near Karl's house, too. But they did not knock on the door. He looked down at them. There were four men. He looked down on their shoulders; on their backs rounded by years of hard work.

They stood there with their burden. The new one. But it was not for Karl Lee to lift it from them.

Mari Lee said:

'Well, now you've started something – '

'It's just a misunderstanding,' he replied. 'I'll go down and tell them that.'

'Ask them to search for Rolf,' she said impulsively. 'No, I'll do it myself!'

She stepped toward the open window to call down. Karl stopped her.

'No, don't.'

'Why not?'

'It would only frighten him if a whole lot of people came after him. Let him take his time.'

She gave it up.

The four men had not moved away. They shifted their stances and remained standing there. A large group of people had gathered over by the barn. And more lights came drifting along the road. The lanterns shone brighter now.

'I'd better go down,' Karl Lee said.

'What are you going to do?'

'Be among them,' he answered resolutely. 'They have a right to that much at least.'

'I'll stay here.'

He went down. The four men were still standing in front of the door. They looked questioningly at him. He knew them all well, but they were somehow changed now. They grew uneasy as he joined them and they said in turn:

'Dark this evening.'

'Wind's changed – '

'Coming from the south.'

'Rain tomorrow.'

Karl Lee nodded. He found no words to use. The four men moved away when he did not answer them and disappeared into a shadow. Karl Lee could hear that there were people on all sides. He went back into the house. Better wait a bit, he thought, as if to gain extra time.

8

INSIDE THE HAY MOW it was almost pitch dark. There were lights in the barnyard outside, but they did not penetrate the towering red wall. No one in there wanted any light. Hill was sitting at one end of the mow and Dale at the other, and somewhere between them was the stretcher – nothing more.

They had not had any contact with each other for a long time until finally Dale's voice sounded out of the darkness:

'Are you still here?'

'Sure I'm here,' the answer came back in Hill's familiar voice. 'And I can stay here if you want to go.'

'No, you can go.'

'You can go home and get some supper if you want to.'

'No, *you* might as well go get some supper. I don't want any.'

They were usually on the best of terms with one another, but now they spoke irritably.

The stretcher lay there between them in the darkness, and they guarded it jealously. It had become theirs. They both wished that the other would leave. Neither wanted to share it with the other, each was waiting until the other could hold out no longer, so that he could stay alone and endure it and hold out and save himself.

'Do they know at home that you're sitting here?'

'Sure. They saw us turn back.'

Useless.

At first they had been proud at having secured for themselves the sacrifice of sitting with the body of the murderer at the expense of all the others who were now repenting their actions elsewhere. It had been a secret comfort to begin with, but it did not last. Now each of them felt he must sit there alone if it were to be any help. Why can't he go?

Beneath their feet was the barn, with stalls and pens for animals and bins for feed and produce. Jens had ample room to store his produce in the huge barn. He could spread the hay out thin to air it if it was not quite dry when he brought it in. The grain bins were still empty, but soon wave after wave of ripe golden grain would be spread there. From the pens and stalls could be heard the stamping of heavy feet and the thud of horns against the wall. The barn was rich and manifold, but Hill and Dale did not notice it now – though at any other time their hearts would have been warmed at the sight.

My heart? My heart is black and vile. Don't mention it.

They heard a cough on the other side of the wall. People were standing close up to it, standing quietly.

Why?

The barn had drawn them. But not with the earthly fruitfulness of which it was a part – rather with the leaden weight it housed this evening. Each man had as it were left his bad conscience there and had now returned to tend to it.

Hill and Dale heard more people arrive. They were not surprised.

The hinges of the double doors screeched, and someone asked carefully into the darkness:

'Is there anyone there?'

Let him ask again.

'Is there anyone there?' he repeated, his voice full of what was weighing on his mind.

They did not make a sound.

Let him ask again.

But this time he did not. Dared not. The silence after each question was too menacing. They heard his steps retreating down the ramp. They had turned him down. We're not handing over anything.

They heard other people arrive. They felt it as a demand upon them, and made themselves hard: we won't hand anything over.

9

ROLF HAD LEFT with but one thought in mind: just to get away from it all. No one here will try to understand me.

He walked along a path toward the woods. The dusk did not come quickly enough for him out in the open. He felt a need to hide himself away, to find something to cover and protect him – and put an end to all this.

He felt it was impossible to continue after what had happened. He would have to go away for good. He could not think clearly about it, for the wild events of the day were still too close and he was still half dazed.

At a turn in the path he ran into one of the neighbors. They both jumped. The neighbor said good evening hastily, shyly. In the mood Rolf was in it only hurt him all the more. People avoid me. He hurried past. But a little later he met a couple walking along together. And farther off he could make out the figure of a woman alone. They were all headed in the same direction. Towards Lee.

He knew the couple and he steeled himself and asked where they were going.

'To Lee,' one of them said, a bit embarrassed at having to say it.

'We were told to come,' the other hurried to add.

''This evening ?' Rolf asked.

'We were told to come,' they repeated and walked on. Away from him.

'That's my home,' Rolf said in a strange tone of voice as they passed him.

It was Gudrun following them. Ivar's wife. But for some reason the couple did not want company. They all looked ashamed.

The couple left Rolf standing there alone. Gudrun approached. She would rather not have met him, that was easy to see. Everyone was that way now. He felt an urge to be nasty to her. It made little difference how he behaved any longer anyway. He could just say whatever he pleased.

'Am I in your way, Gudrun?' he asked, and placed himself in the middle of the narrow path.

She heard his hostile tone of voice, stopped and looked aside, but did not answer.

'You're going to Lee too, I suppose?'

'Yes.'

'Were you told to come?'

'Yes.'

'By my father?' he asked suspiciously.

'By Kari Ness. She's been all over the island, I guess.'

That startled him. But it made no difference to him now. Let her do whatever she wanted.

'Well, what are you just standing there for, Gudrun?' he asked.

She was tormented and troubled enough already and answered in kind:

'I don't have to account to you for anything.'

It just encouraged Rolf. He felt ostracized and full of enmity towards all he met.

'But your husband – isn't he going to Lee this evening too?'

'Rolf, you just stop that now. It's all your fault, so be quiet.'

He replied excitedly:

'Is it all my fault?'

'Wasn't it you who stirred everyone else up?'

'Is that what people are saying?'

'Yes, of course it is. There's nothing else to say about it, either. Now let me past.'

She tried to slip past him, but he blocked the path.

'Wait!' he said.

'Am I going to have to call for help?'

'If you want to. We two are old friends. So you're going to Lee, are you, Gudrun? That's my home – that's what I'm telling everyone I meet. That's my home, and it's strange to see you all going there.'

'Let me past now; someone's coming.'

'Is there anything wrong with that?'

'It's so terrible to stand here talking like this!' she said honestly, and he grew ashamed when he heard it. But he did not move aside for her. Someone was coming up behind her. A man.

'There's no rush,' he said. 'I've got plenty of time now.'

'You?'

'Yes. So you're all gathering together to stone me now.'

'To stone you?'

'Yes, that's what it looks like to me. You said it was all my fault.'

'Yes, and it was. You shouldn't have stirred everyone up like that.'

She said it calmly, but he saw how tormented her face was. Strained and tormented.

'Is that all you have to say as a farewell, Gudrun?'

She did not answer. He began trembling again. It grew dark and stormy around him.

'You can gather at my house and do whatever you want,' he said, 'but you'll not get *me*.'

He stepped aside so that she could pass. She walked away. Quickly. Without looking at him. Frightened. What he had said had only frightened her. She hurried to get out of sight.

It was Ivar following her. Her husband. Rolf stepped aside for him to pass.

'Good evening, Ivar. You'd better hurry and catch up with your wife.'

Ivar stopped. Stood there with his burden. Turned the same shy eyes toward Rolf, eyes that could drive him to something desperate.

'I saw you there, Ivar,' Rolf said threateningly. 'You weren't far away when he died.'

Ivar stood still and blinked his eyes.

'You were at him, too, Ivar.'

'That's why I'm here,' Ivar replied.

Rolf had no answer for this. He made a movement as if to step nearer, but Ivar started off quickly. Rolf saw only his back. Then his back also disappeared.

Rolf stepped across the path and into the woods. I don't want to see any more shy eyes. And no more people.

The woods were thick. And dark. He lay down to rest. I don't want to see any more people. His mind was empty of all other thoughts.

10

'DID YOU SEE HIM ?' Mari Lee asked when her husband came back.

'No. But there are people all over. And more are coming all the time.'

'Hasn't anyone seen him ?'

'Didn't ask.'

She was lighting a candle on the table when he entered. She stared in horror at him when he said this.

'How are you made, Karl ?'

'I couldn't,' he answered in a way that stopped her from making any more accusations against him.

He suddenly noticed how many lamps and candles were burning in the room. And she had just lit another. It made the room easier to enter, as if the dead girl lying there had been lifted.

'What's the idea of all these lights ?' he asked just the same.

'Oh – – – '

She dragged out the word as she lit still another candle. There were many candlesticks on the old farm. She placed the candles and lamps around the room. Her husband looked at her in amazement when he saw how she seemed in this way to lift the room up out of misfortune. That simple room with the pale walls. It was as if these walls were as thin as leaves and the room was floating away like a ship with its cargo.

He did not thank her, but he was thankful when he saw what she had accomplished. It occurred to him that she must now feel childless.

Her face was stiff. Stiffened into a mask that told nothing. But she was aboard the lighted ship.

They stood still and let themselves be carried along.

A knock came at the door. They started.

Jens entered. His face was dark. He did not notice that he had stepped aboard a thin, thin ship. He came from outside where all his neighbors stood lined up against the towering red walls. He was startled by all the light.

'I came with a message from the people outside, Karl,' he said. 'They want to talk to you.'

'But I don't understand – ' Karl Lee replied.

'They asked me to tell you,' Jens continued. 'You said you wanted to talk to them.'

Karl did not answer.

'Didn't you ?'

'Yes, but – '

'They've all been told to come up here this evening.'

'What ? I didn't send for them. No one can say I did, either, because it's not true.'

'Kari Ness has been out telling them,' Jens explained.

'Kari Ness ? I haven't talked to her.'

'She's been in every home on the island.'

Jens did not add what he would have at any other time – that it was just as he thought, just one of her crazy ideas. Instead he told it as something important and decisive. His meeting with the people outside had done that.

They felt how the shadow of Kari Ness rose up inside them. Mari Lee did not move. Jens looked at Karl Lee compellingly.

'You'd better come down, Karl.'

'I don't know what to say to them!' Karl answered in confusion.

'You'd better come down anyway.'

Jens turned. And Karl Lee followed him –
'I'll probably be gone a while, Mari.'
She nodded, her back to them.

11

ROLF WAS STILL sitting somewhere deep in the woods.

Turn around –

He felt as if he were being kept company, although he knew there was no one there. Nothing but his own fear, which took the form of imagining there was someone behind him and forced him to turn around and look.

It was so dark there in the woods that he could just barely make out the shapes around him.

He could still hear steps up on the road. Someone going to Lee, kicking stones he did not see in the darkness. Rolf did not know how long he had been sitting there; perhaps not so long. People going to Lee. That's my home; I know every inch of its ground, and every twig and stone.

There go my neighbors to gather together and place all the blame on me.

But they won't find me.

There was little order in the thoughts that passed through his mind. Suddenly he felt that his companion took form and moved around from behind his back and stood in front of him. Stood facing him. A looming, faceless form in the twilight.

Come, he thought he heard it say. Firmly, but not frighteningly.

Rolf trembled and felt that he had to answer 'yes'.

Well, come along, then.

Rolf became frightened just the same. He said out loud, wretched and distressed as he was:

'Help us poor fools.'

Then he sat quietly again.

There's nothing left for you in life but suffering, it seemed to tell him. And he believed that himself. He was on the point of standing up and walking toward that faceless figure that was waiting for him, walking toward it with hanging, limp arms. He would have been welcomed. Calmly and firmly.

Again it called, still in a friendly tone:

Come along, then.

Yes, but –

There were many things holding him back, that rose up in him in the midst of his despair and were strong. They wakened within him and held him fast.

He was torn between the two forces. But that was stronger which waited patiently for him and called to him in a friendly voice. He felt that all resistance was in vain.

Suddenly a dry twig cracked close by him. A dry twig under a foot.

He jumped up.

The faceless figure disappeared.

Are they after me here, too? If they can't understand me they could at least leave me in peace.

He wanted to run.

No, I'll just stay and tell them what I think when they get here.

Whoever it was approached leisurely, finally took form out of the dusk and turned out to be a woman. Kari Ness.

What does she want? I don't want to have anything to do with her. Is she going to drag me home? His thoughts criss-crossed. He was afraid of her.

It appeared that she was looking for him, for she walked straight up to him and said:

'Is it here you've been hiding?'

'Yes; so what?' Rolf answered wearily.

'I have a message for you, Rolf. I've been looking for you.'

'I don't want any message from anyone,' Rolf replied. He was afraid of Kari Ness for the first time in his life. She stood before him formidable and mighty. He answered evasively, but she had burst the mood he had been sitting and weaving around himself. He felt alone.

Kari Ness said:

'Lee's your home, isn't it?'

'Yes; so what?'

It startled him that she used the same phrase he himself had used against Gudrun and Ivar. Kari Ness did not say it as a question. She knew perfectly well where he lived. She only affirmed it.

'Well, then it's best you go home,' she said. 'That's the message I have for you.'

'Who from?'

'It's a message I've been bearing around the island,' she answered.

'Have my parents sent you?'

'No, they haven't sent me. But come along now and follow me home.'

'I don't have anything to do there,' he said defiantly. She was not *only* strong, this strange woman standing before him. She was usually shy and retiring, and a bit of this broke through even now. But today she possessed remarkable power. There was something about her that was not her own.

'It's *here* you don't have anything to do,' she said. 'You mustn't throw yourself away.'

You have no right to preach to me, he felt like saying, but did not. Instead he began to walk away slowly. Her power suddenly increased.

'Stop, I say!'

'Who do you think you are?' he shouted furiously.

She looked into his face. She had stepped close to him and said in alarm:

'I'm so afraid for all who leave us –'

She did not tell him to stop any more – he had not tried to move again. He did not understand her face. She was as tall as he was and the stern features of her face were right before his eyes. It was a beautiful face. Rolf could remember when it had been both laughing and beautiful. Before her husband and sons had perished at sea.

He saw that her eyes were large and shining in the twilight. She was so near that he could see it. It was a rare sight. They could not always be like that. This evening they were shining and large.

She said:

'You just ran off without having thought about it at all.'

'Haven't I ?'

'No, or you wouldn't have left.'

Rolf said:

'There's nothing left for me after what happened today. So there's nothing for me to do but leave.'

'And make everything even worse,' she added.

'I don't want to torment anyone with the sight of me! And *I* don't want to be tormented, either.'

'Well, come along home now,' Kari Ness said as if she had heard nothing he had been saying.

Rolf did not move. Could not take a step either backwards or forwards, despite his bold words. He no longer had strength to flee.

'Did you hear me, Rolf ?'

'No!'

He was afraid when he said it, but he had to add:

'Just who do you think you are running around this evening and giving orders and sticking your nose in everybody's business ?'

She did not answer that. She was so tall and formidable now, as it grew darker, that it was unnecessary. She had great power now.

He had to continue, to defy her, wound her and weaken her:

'You're not even all there,' he said viciously.

His words struck Kari Ness like a blow, the kind that injures deeply but leaves no outward mark.

Rolf felt immediately how he had lost to her, but could not stop:

'Everyone knows you're not all there.'

He could see how deeply he injured her. She answered without hesitating:

'That's just what frightens me so much.'

'What ?'

'That I don't know what I am. If I only had as much faith as a seed of mustard, Rolf, I wouldn't be frightened the least bit.'

He said nothing.

'Why do you try to hurt me, Rolf ?'

He still said nothing.

'They all believed in me this evening when I told them to go to Lee,' she said. 'Almost all of them – '

'Yes, I saw that. What are they going to do there ?'

'They're longing for company,' she answered, unsure of herself. 'And you're going, too. Rolf!'

'Yes ?'

'I know I just wander around. But I can't help it.'

She added in consternation and despair:

'I've lost them!'

Her words shook Rolf. She continued, gathering strength for a challenge to him:

'Go home, Rolf, and take whatever the future brings. I beg you to, and I've lost sons myself.'

He felt it as a compelling invitation. He wanted to be able to see it like that and surrender himself to it. There was something tempting lying hidden in her words. Life. Had he really ever thought of running away from it all ? He no longer was so sure.

He surrendered to the challenge. He belonged at Lee.

'No one understands me there,' he said. 'I've asked and asked them to try to ever since it happened.'

'Come along now,' was all she replied.

He felt like asking: But can you understand me, Kari Ness ? but could not get the words out. She had come looking for him, that was something. She would have found me no matter where I had hidden! he thought. She said:

'Now we'll go to Lee where you were born.'

'I don't know what there is for me to do there any longer.'

'Yes, you do.'

Yes, I do, he thought.

'We have to be there like everybody else,' she said. 'There's no use thinking anything else.'

They began to go. Kari Ness loomed large on the path in front of him. He thought about how she had appeared to the island's people this evening, risen up before them on the road, in their yards, their houses, wherever they were, and called to them. It was not surprising that they all had responded. But was she quite sane? There was no way to know. What had happened to her had given her great power.

They came to the road and headed for Lee, quickly, resolutely.

There was no one on the road now. Everyone who intended to had arrived at Lee. It was dark and still. Who is this I'm walking beside?

I'll probably never know. She's transformed. There's no holding back when she calls –

The leaves brushed against their faces now and then. A myriad of plants stood in the dark and sent out their fragrances. The farms they passed were dark. A dull roaring from the sea reached their ears.

Inga is long since dead now.

He stopped short at the thought, as if to look for the meaning behind it. He found none.

He could barely see the dark-clad widow beside him in the darkness. She strode along in silence. Now she was waiting for him to start walking again and finally said impatiently:

'Aren't you coming, Rolf?'

'Yes, yes.'

'There's no use stopping now. You'll just have to take what's coming.'

They passed a small home at the side of the road. Two small houses. Indescribably deserted – because it was Kari Ness' home. There were many signs of decay about it. Even if they could not be seen in the darkness those who passed knew they were there.

They walked past quickly.

Towards Lee. There lies the stranger in the barn, dead. The barn at Lee would be the center of everything this evening.

Rolf, you killed him.

I wasn't the only one –

Everyone's pointed you out.

They strode along. The darkness fell closer around them. It was still hot. A raw breeze blew in from the marshes. Oh! he stepped on something slippery that cried out softly and strangely. He had stepped on a frog. They often crawled out of the ditches in the twilight and sat on the road just there.

Kari Ness said:

'Look at all the lights up at Lee!'

Yes, it was light up there. The barnyard was only faintly lit up by the lantern hung out as usual, but rays of light streamed out of the barn on all sides. And up in the house two windows shone with a radiant light. Rolf shivered when he saw it, for he knew which room it was.

He took it all in. This is my home. It's good I came back. I'd better go up to the barn.

Kari Ness slipped into the darkness and was gone.

12

KARL LEE WAS STANDING beside the ramp leading up to the mow talking to Jens and a couple of other men.

He and Jens had left the shining, sailing room up in the house.

The barn gleamed at them when they stepped out into the yard. More light was pouring out of it than Karl had ever seen before since they were not in the habit of leaving lanterns lit throughout the whole building.

On any other day he would have been filled with joy at the sight of the barn he had built and which the light that now streamed out through all its windows and cracks showed off so well. The people who had come had hung their lanterns up inside.

Not every window was filled with light. The windows of the cow barn were dark, for no one had gone in and disturbed the cows. And it appeared to be dark up in the mow, at the heart of everything, where Hill and Dale were sitting. All was extinguished and oppressive there.

It was not a building to be ashamed of as it stood there witnessing to a youthful surge of power.

'That's strange,' Karl Lee said as soon as he came out of the house and saw it.

Jens was in front of him and turned around:

'What's strange?'

He asked almost as if Karl Lee had committed a sin. They all felt hostile toward him – because they had taken part in the chase. They had offered themselves for his family. That was, at any rate, how they tried to see it. Jens had met this attitude in some of those who had come to Lee and had taken it for his own. It helped a bit. What's strange?

'Just how the light is streaming out of my barn,' Karl Lee answered. 'What's going on in there, anyway, Jens?'

'They're waiting for you.'

Karl made no reply to that. He did not feel he could possibly face them.

'You said you wanted to talk to us!' Jens said.

'Yes, I know, but – '

He noticed how Jens included himself in the mob.

Talk to them?

What could he say that they would want to hear? He wanted to do only one thing: shout to everyone who was there and ask: Have you seen my son?

Two men stepped out of the shadow of the ramp and said 'good evening' in worried voices. They were not antagonistic; just worried and worn-out.

'Good evening,' Karl Lee replied. 'Are you two here?'

'Yes, we were told to come.'

'Yes, of course,' Karl Lee said.

They began to talk about crops and the weather and the sea. That brought them rest. There were various traces of the sows' battle in the barnyard earlier in the day. A broken fence and other marks that showed up in the lamp light – but Jens did not say a word about it, gave no explanation. Occasional grunts came from the pig pens, fewer than could be expected at this time of day. A cow inside the barn lowed. The huge building was filled with restlessness this evening. The four men heard it, but pretended not to notice. They talked nervously together about the weather and the good crops to come.

Karl Lee was standing so that the light fell upon him, and several people came toward him. A group of five or six. They stopped and said good evening.

Karl Lee stood there in silence. He was afraid of these people. They asked:

'What are we supposed to do?'

They all knew that it was Kari Ness who had brought them together, but no one spoke her name. She was an unrelenting voice that cut through them and which they could not bring themselves to mention.

'Let's go up here,' Karl Lee said and started up the ramp to the mow.

They looked at him in horror.

'What are we going to do there?'

'Come on; we'll all go in,' Karl Lee replied, sternly, commandingly.

They were filled with reluctance, but still went – because in reality they wanted to. Something within them wanted to. He who was lying in there had become a part of them since they had laid their hands on him. They followed Karl Lee up the ramp.

He opened one of the large double doors. It was dark inside. A lantern somewhere down below penetrated only the outer edge of darkness.

'Are you still sitting there?' Karl Lee called in to Hill and Dale, just in case they were still there.

Since he was the owner of the farm they answered quickly. But did not move.

The others followed Karl Lee into the mow. Carefully. He must be lying somewhere in the middle. They spread out and lost all contact with one another. It was good that no lanterns had been hung up in here, so that no one saw them as they stood there longing to do penance.

From down below they heard the shuffling of feet and mumbling. Brusque exchanges of words. They could also hear that the animals were awake and uneasy. The barn was spacious and restless. Every man could go off by himself. Some wandered into far corners of the big barn. There was no way of knowing how many people were there. Then Karl Lee's voice sounded out. He asked into the darkness, gropingly:

'Has anyone seen my son?'

It sounded frail. There in the darkness he could not resist the urge to ask that question. He did not now need to look anyone in the face while he asked.

'When do you mean?' someone asked back.

'*Now*, of course.'

'No, we haven't seen him now.'

They were on the point of adding: we saw him in the orchard. Those who felt they needed a scapegoat. And the darkness helped one man express it. He said to Karl Lee whom he did not see:

'We wouldn't have been in on this if Rolf hadn't stirred us up to it.'

'Well, it's too late to talk about that,' Karl Lee replied. 'When you've been in on it, you've been in on it. I realize that's why you're here.'

A voice said stubbornly:

'We did what was right.'

'No!' Karl Lee replied.

Someone left. Someone who had no reason to stay any longer, someone who had not come to repent. Those who stayed were glad they were not in his shoes.

It became deathly quiet. An ugly roar rose up from the pig pens; so ugly that it must have been the boar. It came as from below the surface of the earth. The barn seemed to collapse around them.

Karl Lee went out quickly, down toward the sound.

13

THERE WAS USUALLY peace and quiet over the pig pens in the evening. All the pigs lay there and sighed and slept deeply, and the flies no longer buzzed. Only the sour smell was as it was during the day.

It had grown quiet this evening, too, despite the tumult with the sows earlier in the day. The tiny motherless pigs had crawled around and squeaked – but then evening came and sleep took them as firmly as on all previous evenings, and they fell asleep in a heap. The sow that had eaten her young had returned to those that were left. She had regained her senses and gave them to suck and fell asleep with them. Bergit had worked at calming her while Jens and Helga joined the chase. Then came the terrible scene at the wall outside, after which Jens and Helga came into the house, horrified and with smarting consciences.

But peace settled over the pig pens. The outside pens were empty, the boar's pen as well. His wasteland was deserted; he had disappeared through the narrow, dirtied door that led to his pen inside. His door was the darkest thing on the farm in the evening.

This evening the peace was broken by man. Most of the adults on the island came to the barn. Some of them had, of course, locked themselves in and refused to heed the call when it came. Mothers who had children to watch did not come, either, and the larger children were forbidden to join the adults. But there were still many people who came, and the degree of their need varied greatly, determined by factors not readily apparent. The events of the day had been the last touch that had brought them to violence. They had killed an unfortunate fellow human being.

Bow your heads, said a voice within those who were most weighed down. And they bowed their heads and entered. Who are you? the voice asked again. The question pursued them and buzzed around their head like flies around an open wound.

Come along, Kari Ness had said to them in the midst of their confusion. Come to Lee.

What will we do there? What good will that do? But they came when it grew dark. They disappeared into the barn one by one. There was room for them all.

Some even crept into the pig pens in the dusk, into that darkest corner of the barn to bow down in the dust. They were the humblest people on the island. Now they were crushed and cowed.

They found their way to the pig pens, though they themselves did not know why. Here I lie in the dust and am the most worthless being in creation.

They bumped into the pigs. The pigs woke up and grunted in annoyance. Some of them became afraid and stood and whined as pigs do in the face of danger. The wretched people heard the whining as they opened their hearts to the unknown force they were seeking.

One man came too close to the boar. He wanted to be alone, and groped his way into the pen. He floundered around in the rancid smell and the inky darkness and dragged his feet through the saw-dust spread on the floor until he suddenly kicked the boar in the

E

snout as he lay by the wall. The boar jumped up with a harsh grunt. The man jumped also, backwards. They stood there in the darkness, terrified of each other. The boar's dark and pitted brow was hidden to the man, who only heard a low grunting that nailed him to the spot.

It did not last long. The boar had to put an end to the terror riding him, he bellowed loudly and charged blindly. His clouded eyes saw nothing in the darkness but he heard the man breathing, and charged and slashed.

The man screamed as he was struck and thrown aside like a tuft of wool, his foot gashed by the boar's tusks. The boar struck his brow against the wall and stood there grunting in rage and fear. Fear was always lurking in his cramped brain, ready to loosen his wildest instincts. He charged and struck again, but this time his tusks missed their unseen mark. He swung his head viciously and struck a glancing blow that threw the man against a post, head first.

He crawled to his feet and clung to the post, unable to come farther. He tried to collect his shaken senses. The boar grunted close by him.

The door was thrown open and people came running in. Karl Lee entered carrying a lantern at arm's length.

'What's going on in here?' he shouted.

The man stood and blinked at the light, still groggy after the blow.

'Where am I?' he muttered.

'In my barn.'

The man could not quite grasp it.

The boar stopped grunting when the light came. He stood there silent and lowering.

'Did he hurt you? Come over here,' Karl Lee said and pulled the man out of the pen and over to a faucet.

'Here's water.'

The man stuck his head under the stream of water. His foot was only scratched. His trouser leg had suffered most.

The door squeaked. Jens came in. He had also heard the bellowing and it was he who owned the pigs. He had had enough trouble with them already that day.

'He's just been scratched up a bit by the boar,' Karl Lee explained.

'They don't have to go in *there*,' Jens said irritably and went out again.

Now Karl Lee saw that there were people in the other pig pens as well, people who shrank back from the light he had brought. It shocked him to see how they tried to hide away from all human eyes.

'Come out,' he said to them.

He said it respectfully.

But they did not come out. Only the man who had been injured by the boar stood there in the light washing himself. He let the cold water clear his head. The others just shrank back into the corners of the pens.

Karl Lee was at a loss for what to do. He felt he had sacrificed these people for his daughter and a wave of guilt swept over him.

'Please come out,' he repeated. 'Let's talk this all over, since we've been called together.'

'We don't have anything to talk about,' someone answered in a choked voice.

No one else made a sound. They huddled down and wished he would go out again. Take that light away! The boar stood by the wall, motionless, trying to dig a thought out of the darkness in his brain.

Karl Lee said:

'Please don't take it like that.'

No answer.

'I realize you did it for my daughter,' he continued.

But they did not expect anything of him and let their eyes fall. They bowed down in the dust, expecting nothing.

Karl Lee stood before them in silence, powerless to thank them, as they turned away from him and sank down in darkness and hopelessness again.

'Please leave now, Karl,' one of them said – softly. It had the effect of a forceful command on him. He let the lantern sink down at his side, and left. The last thing he saw was the boar, still standing in the same position, his brow dark and pitted.

14

AT ABOUT THIS TIME Rolf entered the barn, uncertain as to his mission there, but with a feeling that he could not stay away. The contents of the barn had drawn him – just as it had drawn all the others. He saw the light in the room where his mother was sitting, but went past the house and into the secret barn. Lonesome lanterns hung here and there, left by people who had used them to find their way in and then had not blown them out. He met a couple of women who turned away when they saw him. This made him want to speak to them, and he called one of them by name:

'Christine – '

She pretended not to hear.

'Is my father in here?'

She just shook her head.

'That's a fine way to behave,' he said disrespectfully, and immediately regretted the words. This was no ordinary meeting of people, he was fully aware of that. It was their hope, and their horror, and shame and regret that were meeting here. It had swollen up today, and broken and overflowed. They had seen themselves, and the sight had been dismaying. It had driven them to this groping about in the barn at Lee – there where the dead man lay like a leaden weight and crushed everything to the earth.

Look at those two women – all the others must be just the same. He started to walk on. Then one of them said to his back:

'Rolf – '

'Yes?'

'Aren't you afraid ?'

'We are,' the other woman added.

He heard that they included him and did not set a boundary between them and him. He wanted to thank them for that. He did not answer their question, for it had not been asked like that.

'Your father's here,' one of them told him.

Rolf left them. What's Dad going to do ? he thought. It must be him they've come to make demands of.

Rolf had seen the barn every day of his life. It was so familiar to him that he really did not see it, nor how large it was. Every board and post, and every piece of equipment was known to him. Even in the dark he knew where everything was. His studying had not cancelled what he had learned in his childhood, he had spent too many days playing in the barn for that.

It was just so weirdly unrecognizable this evening with all these silent people standing there waiting for his father.

And I'm looking for him, too, he thought. Not mother this time. Now only Dad can help me.

He came upon a group of men around a lantern by the door to the hay chute. He saw their hostility toward him. Another blow. He braced himself and asked if they had seen his father.

'No,' one of them answered.

Rolf walked on. He thought he saw Else and Gudrun standing together at one spot. They also turned away quickly. Else's out of reach now, he thought. He had seen how something froze in her when he told her the truth earlier that evening.

He ran into Jens.

'Oh, is it you ?' Jens said. 'Have you come back ?'

Rolf could hear that Jens was thinking of other things.

'Yes, I came back.'

'I've got to stay here and keep an eye on all this,' Jens said. 'I should have gone to bed long ago.'

Rolf knew that Jens was just trying to cover up. He was as much a part of it as all the others.

'Have you seen my father?'

'He's looking for you. At least he's asking everyone if they've seen you anywhere.

It would be difficult to meet him. Jens came to his aid.

'Come along with me, Rolf,' Jens said. They were standing near the door to the horse stable.

Jens and Rolf were old friends. Rolf had as a boy been able to get many things from Jens that he was denied by his father. Perhaps it was the memory of all these moments that made Jens feel their old comradeship now.

'Let's go in to Black Lady,' Jens suggested, suddenly seized by a happy thought.

The black mare was the apple of Jens' eye. The idea appealed to Rolf. Yes! he thought, let's go in to Black Lady. There we can feel safe.

There was no one in there. The people who had come to the barn had not entered and disrupted the stables. It was part of their way of thinking that these animals had to have peace and quiet at night. It was dark in there and they could hear the mare standing in her stall.

Now they too stood there, in the dark, the door shut behind them.

Jens was probably secretly stroking Black Lady. Rolf leaned against a post.

A while passed in silence. They heard the restlessness outside.

Jens cleared his throat:

'Did you hear me say that your father's asking everybody if they've seen you?'

'Yes, I heard it. But he can't help me, Jens.'

'Perhaps not, but – maybe you should go and tell him you're here anyway.'

'Do you think that's so easy?' Rolf asked.

'No, but it's hardest for your father, you know. But wait until you feel that you can.'

Rolf did not answer. He felt the nearness of Black Lady, and connected it with the smell of the hay outside. He thought about how little consolation it in reality was to have studied and thought and struggled so much and found so many things important and *made* so many things important when one was as lost as he was. At that moment he did not find it worth as much as so simple and childish a thing as the nearness of a large, still horse dozing in the darkness.

Jens cleared his throat again. Asked carefully:

'How is it for you?'

There was nothing insistent about the way he asked it. Instead it opened closed doors and made it easier for Rolf.

'Terrible,' he replied.

They felt the pressing weight above their heads somewhere in the hay mow. Jens stood stroking Black Lady and thought that Rolf did not notice it. Jens was greatly changed now from what he was just a short while before when he had come to fetch Karl Lee.

Black Lady stood stock still under Jens' caressing hand. Jens finally asked, hoarsely and in bewilderment:

'What'll I do, Rolf? I was there too.'

'I can't tell you,' Rolf answered.

'No, that's true.'

'The police will come and get *me*,' Rolf said. 'So I know what's waiting for me.'

'Yes, I guess they will.'

'They've been sent for, haven't they?'

'Yes,' Jens answered, 'that's what I've heard. They'll be here in the morning.'

Rolf confessed:

'I'd thought of not showing up.'

'No –'

'But then Kari Ness asked me to come back.'

'Oh. So she's been after you, too.'

Jens spoke softly and respectfully. He didn't want to talk about Kari Ness any more, that was easy to hear. Her name tore at what he was struggling with. He added quickly:

'You'd better go find your father and mother now, Rolf.'

Rolf felt the words as a hard hand trying to throw him out of the only place he had found a little peace.

'Yes,' he said. 'But it's not so easy!'

'No, but you'd better go. It's not so easy for them to wait, either.'

There was no way to avoid it any longer. Rolf guessed that Jens wanted to be alone in there. That was one reason why he was so insistent. Jens is just like all the others. I'm the only one being tossed back and forth. It was too much for him, because Jens had no more to share with him, and he shouted out:

'Can you tell me what I'm going to do!'

Black Lady jumped violently at Rolf's agonized cry.

'Shhh,' Jens said, 'you'll frighten Black Lady.'

He found the door latch, and opened it. Light from a lantern flickered in.

'Go out and find your father,' Jens said. 'He's here somewhere. I'm having a hard enough time with myself, Rolf. That's just how it is.'

He was the older of them, and worked half of the farm. Rolf left. Jens closed the door and stayed inside. It was as if Jens had buried himself, and now refused to come back to life. No, not like that. He was standing with a faithful friend and comrade and servant, opening his weary heart, and longing to repent.

Jens was there in the stable – others were elsewhere. In corners. In the pig pens. Everywhere in the restless, transformed barn. Up in the mow lies a weight that is crushing us.

Rolf saw it all in sudden flashes. And there'll come a day when all who have hidden themselves in their graves will hear a strident voice – he tried to shake it out of his mind, but it stuck fast.

He suddenly stood face to face with Else, to whom he had lied. She was standing in a narrow passageway and he could not slip by.

'Are you here too, Else?'

She just looked at him. Searchingly. Her eyes grew large.

'What's the matter?' he asked.

She did not answer. Just looked at him. He was shocked by it. It was so grotesque. She wanted to know the full truth about him. Didn't she realize yet that it was all over ?

'Can't you speak any longer, Else ?'

At any rate she did not. He did not know if he was seeing right. Was he dreaming ? She turned and walked away.

Was it she, or what was it ? Of course it was she. She stood and looked at me to try to find out how a liar takes it.

He began trembling. He walked farther along the passageway. He saw some people up ahead. He stepped into a corner where apparently no one wished to stand, but jumped back quickly: there lay Kari Ness on a large over-turned crate, sleeping. She lay there curled up, the picture of poverty and exhaustion, overtaken by sleep. Her shoes were much too large.

He remained standing there, clutching a post and staring entranced at the sleeping figure.

15

KARL LEE FOUND ROLF standing there beside Kari Ness a little while later. He was wandering around, at a loss as to what he should do for the people to whom he felt indebted and who had found their way to his barn unsummoned by him. This problem was so pressing now that it even pushed his anxiety for Rolf into the background. The sorrow caused by Inga's death was like a part of himself that had been swept away by an avalanche. Now it had grown still, and nameless. It was so recent that it was still numb. But both that and his concern for Rolf were his own personal problems and he could shut them off within himself.

But these neighbors! What should he do about them ? He saw that they were measuring him in the lamplight. They stood there, wretched and repenting, but still waiting for something from him.

That undoubtedly was one of the reasons they had come so quickly when Kari Ness had taken it upon herself to call them.

Look, there's Rolf.

Rolf's come back!

A wave of relief swept over him.

'Ah, there you are, Rolf,' he said calmly.

Rolf was also struggling with himself, and just had to plunge into it:

'Yes, we were called to your barn,' he said.

'It would seem so – ' Karl Lee replied.

He saw Kari Ness lying there asleep. He was startled, but all he said was:

'So she's fallen asleep now. What could have made her so tired?'

They stood looking at her. It was in a way a relief that she was sleeping a little while. Her long legs were finally at rest. Her mouth no longer spoke disturbing words. She was beautiful as she lay there, she who had arranged this all this evening. It appeared to have been exhausting work.

Was she really quite sane?

Karl Lee was so tormented by concern for the people who had gathered in his barn that a feeling close to hostility toward Kari Ness rose up in him and he felt a need to speak harshly to her. He was tempted to wake her and call her to account – although he had just felt relieved that she was quiet and harmless a while. But she was left to sleep on. They looked at her, and then walked away.

'It was fine that you came back, Rolf. We were worried.'

'Oh, it probably doesn't help much that I came back,' Rolf answered.

'Have you been up to see your mother?'

'No.'

'Come then, we'll go up together. She's worried sick that you'll do something foolish.'

He said it as if it were urgent.

'We might as well, I guess,' Rolf replied. It was all no less difficult just because he had come back. It solved nothing; but it gave strength.

They left the barn as quickly as possible, past people standing on all sides. We're still here, their eyes said. But there were also many who never looked up; the turmoil within them was too great. That afternoon a flaming wildness had spread from man to man. Now afterwards, there in the towering barn, repentance and self-examination spread just as rapidly among them, like a storm that could neither be heard nor seen but which sapped their strength more than anything had ever done before.

Rolf stopped in the yard.

'She's lit an awful lot of lights up there.'

'Yes, she's used every candle in the house.'

They stomped up the dark stairs. It was easy to hear that someone was coming.

Mari Lee opened the door and the light cascaded down toward them. She asked down the staircase:

'Is that you, Karl?'

'Yes, Rolf's here.'

'Is he really -- ?'

They entered the room. She said:

'He really is. Thank God!'

Rolf looked around in amazement. When one entered the room from outside it was like stepping into the heart of a flower. The body of the young girl lying there was no terrifying, crushing weight.

Rolf stood before his mother. Looked at her defiantly. Then he noticed that she was able to look at him now and was no longer shy in his presence.

'It was good you came back,' she said.

Rolf did not answer. She continued:

'What are we going to do now – now that you've come back?'

Rolf answered:

'Oh, I expect the police will take care of that.'

She started, but quickly calmed herself again.

'Yes, I guess so. Thank you for coming back.'

They remained standing there in silence. The room was far, far away somewhere, sailing into the night. They stood there and were a part of its journey for a little while.

Not for long. A knock came at the door. They turned wearily and said 'come in'.

Kari Ness entered. Of course. They hadn't really thought they could escape her.

'Good evening,' she said to Mari Lee.

Mari Lee walked toward her.

'Have you come to us, Kari Ness?'

'Yes, I have an errand with your husband.'

She turned to Karl Lee:

'You'd better come back down to the barn.'

Yes, he felt where he belonged now. He nodded.

Kari Ness looked stiffly at Mari Lee and said:

'They've left me, too!'

Mari Lee said nothing. Just looked at Kari Ness, who continued:

'What do you believe about the bird that falls to earth?'

Mari Lee was still not able to answer.

'If one could only have faith in that,' Kari Ness continued in despair.

Then her moment of weakness passed. She turned to Karl Lee again:

'Come along now. We saw that you left. But you belong there with us.'

Once more she had great power. She stood before them large and stern and cleaved the light-filled room like a dark stake. There was no refusing her.

Karl Lee began to leave.

Rolf also wanted to go. His mother tried to stop him:

'Stay here with us, Rolf.'

'No, not just now.'

He felt as if this room were not for him. He followed his father. Kari Ness went out last.

Mari Lee was left standing alone on the shining ship of her own making.

16

IN THE MOW THE HAY LAY in swelling green mounds and valleys. There was so much room that Jens did not have to pile and tramp the hay, but could just throw the loads off loosely.

There were many people in there now.

They had not taken any lanterns in with them because of the danger of fire. Only a little light came in through the windows from lanterns outside.

There were very many people in there – when one's eyes became used to the dimness.

They could hear Jens' cows moving around in their stalls and objecting to the restlessness that filled the barn. Perhaps someone had gone in there after all.

Karl Lee walked past. They straightened up. Then he was gone.

The air in the mow was filled with spices, but they did not notice it, did not notice what a wonderful room they were in.

In the middle of the mow, where death lay, it was still. Hill and Dale were sitting there, and perhaps still more people. It must have been impossible to breathe there. Isn't he coming back? Karl Lee.

A shadow passed by, in front of a door, momentarily shading a lantern. Karl Lee. No, he didn't stop. His shadow, large and distorted, swept across a wall as he moved away. He was off to another part of the barn.

How is he taking it?

They pushed the thought aside.

One man stood up and said, as loudly as he dared with such a bad conscience:

'Maybe we should go now.'

He got no answer, and sank back down among his hidden feelings. No one left.

But Rolf, then; where's he? He who led us into disaster.

But even if they thought about Rolf now they could no longer feel any resentment toward him. They did not dare to any longer.

An ugly sound came from the direction of the pig pens. A shock ran through the whole barn, from man to man: the boar is loose. He's loose among us –

No one had seen him or met him, but everyone knew it at once, and felt it: the boar's among us.

Don't move! He's dangerous.

They listened breathless.

They had, to be sure, never heard that this boar was vicious. But someone said it softly now, and it was believed before his mouth was shut again. And they had all seen him in his pen. They had no desire to meet him in the dark and feel his vile breath against them. What will I do when he comes? When he touches me?

The boar did not come. They waited and listened. No one saw him. Perhaps it was just a false rumor. They could not be sure. Then someone called to his neighbor:

'Look! There he is.'

'Who? The boar?'

'No, Rolf.'

They saw something pass in front of a lantern. Something indistinct. But someone saw it and shuddered: Rolf is walking around among us and the boar is with him. – They're among us.

It was told without words. Nothing was impossible any longer in that barn. Nothing unbelievable.

Rolf and the boar are walking among us –

17

FINALLY A VOICE sounded out – from a spot from which it reached to many parts of the barn. It was Karl Lee's voice.

'You've all come to my barn – '

There was no strength in his voice. It was uncertain and lonely. But nevertheless it cut through the web of supposition and whispering and reached all of them.

They straightened up, wherever they were. The sound of people turning toward Karl Lee swept through the barn. No sound came down from the mow, but his voice could be heard as plainly there as anywhere else. The crushing weight became even greater because nothing moved up there.

'Can you hear me?' Karl Lee asked.

'Yes,' came the answer from several directions. The only people who could not hear him were those in the pig pens. Nor was any message sent to them.

Karl Lee stood before them, overwhelmed by a great feeling of hopelessness. He had lost much that day – and still he was in debt to these people. To the whole island. He had let them wait. He had gone from corner to corner in the barn and seen how they were waiting for something from him.

They would just have to wait a while longer; there was nothing else to do.

Yes, we're listening, they had answered. It grew breathlessly quiet. Karl Lee said:

'Well, all I can say is that *I* have nothing for you. I know you're expecting something, but I can't give it to you.'

A man far off said:

'That's a bit strange.'

'No, it's not,' Karl Lee replied.

'We think so,' answered the man. 'We think that's a strange thing for you to say.'

'I owe you nothing!' Karl Lee said.

He had just barely enough strength to say it, exhausted as he was.

'You all had the wildness within you,' he continued.

'Well,' said the man over in his corner, 'you're not supposed to argue with people who've suffered a great loss, but we feel you could have met us with something else.''

'I don't have anything to account to you for,' Karl Lee answered.

'No, I can hear that.'

Then there was silence again. No one else took part in the discussion. Karl Lee clutched the post he was standing beside and felt that he had to answer:

'You've been standing here and waiting a long time this evening. Waiting for me. I've felt that. But you'll just have to keep on waiting. I have nothing more to say.'

It grew still.

Kari Ness was not mentioned. She was hard and inflexible. No one knew as well as they themselves, each single one of them, what it was that had brought them there. But they had to hold out to the last – as long as they still possessed a spark of defiance and stubbornness.

No more voices sounded out of the dark corners. Karl Lee began to think that perhaps he had been wrong and that these defiant voices did not speak for everyone there. They could have been exceptions, belonging to those trying to save their own skins. He heard that several people left, those who felt that they had done what was right that afternoon. They had nothing more to do there.

'Well, I have no more to say,' Karl Lee repeated, and groped his way back out of sight. He was an old, trembling man at that moment.

Someone called after him in alarm:

'Karl! Are you leaving us ?'

He did not answer.

Those who had pulled themselves together now lost their resolution. Despair came in its stead. Each man would have to account to himself, without help from any other.

18

I CAN'T –

Karl Lee stood in the darkness and felt the huge barn weighing down on him with crushing force. It was he who had put it there, and now it was full of his neighbors – people who had been driven there by horror at their own deeds, and who had a right to come to precisely that place and fill it with their sorrows.

It was my daughter they were trying to avenge.

The urge tore at him to stand up and shout thank you, thank you for letting yourselves be swept along! I was her father and I thank you all for showing in that way what she meant to you. It's a great consolation for me.

He hid it from them, and swallowed it down, not daring to say it.

At the same time everything he had thought, and read, and learned now demanded that he stand up and condemn their behavior. Violence, wildness, brutality. It was inexcusable that they had let the wild beast within them run loose. Stand up and say it!

He could not, but swallowed that down, too.

You're not doing your duty toward everything you've believed in, and that others have believed in and dreamed of and fought for.

But I can't. I can't do more than I have done. Call it what you will.

Are you *so* weak?

Yes, I am.

He felt wretched, and unworthy. He stood like the others, lonely against the wall.

Now it was night.

Why can't you?
He knew why:
Because Rolf's come back.

If someone had carried Rolf in cold and stiff he would have stood up and condemned it all. In a voice of stone. And condemned Rolf once more: I did what I should have today when I condemned his behavior, even though he died because of it.

He would have said it over Rolf's body. He saw it before him: he would have stood up and said that he had done what he knew was right.

That was the answer: Rolf cold and dead. What sort of an answer was that? Mari would have asked him that. What sort of answer did you get for your hardness, Karl?

How would he feel then? He would have had to agree: yes, what sort of answer did I get? – All he could have replied was: help this wretched man who got such an answer.

Then it would have grown darker around him.

He saw it all as clearly before him as if it had happened.

– But Rolf *was* there, alive. He had turned and come back and was now somewhere in the barn. That made all the difference.

And so you've shirked your duty, and kept silent.

I didn't thank them! I told them they would get nothing from me.

Are you sure that was enough?

No –

He wanted to go to the pig pens, to his humble neighbors there, to those who had bowed down in the filth and had no other thought than to do penance for their wildness and brutality.

He did not go. It wouldn't have helped. He was not made like them, had not so humble and repentant a nature.

19

THE AUGUST NIGHT settled down over the barn at Lee. It was pitch dark outside. A thick mat of clouds had covered the sky and shut out all light. The wind from the south that the men had told Karl Lee about had died down. From the sea came a dull murmuring – that only told how lonely it was to live there.

A fragrance came from the hidden orchard. In the heat of the day the murderer had lain there crushed to the ground. The fruit on the trees kept on slowly ripening. Night and day without pause. From the sea came the taste of salt through the darkness.

Only stripes of light here and there disclosed where the barn was. It blended into the darkness with all its gables and ramps and towering walls.

Deepest night. But no one went home. Those who were still there wanted to be there. They had been forced out of their daily routine and their consciences had driven them to the barn, in a procession fed from many clouded sources.

Karl Lee had turned them down.

They had known he would, and now grew uneasy and crept away. That they were all gathered under one roof after their joint downfall of the day gave rise to a strange draft through the barn, and through them. It was all so different from any other day. It was as if they were waiting for Kari Ness to stride from one end of the barn to the other calling out something she had never told them before, something that would rip them open and cast them down, and burn out that which they longed to be freed from.

She did not come. They did not hear her familiar, wearying voice. They had caught a fleeting glimpse of her, but she had left. She had nothing to tell them. Her mouth was sealed.

But go on home, then! they told themselves, and stop sitting here in the barn like a fool.

They looked around for someone who could leave first and break the spell. No, no one appeared to be willing to.

Well, you go, then. Someone has to be first.

They told themselves that, but sat or stood motionless, afraid to step out of their shadows and show themselves, afraid to hear their steps on the floor. They couldn't move. They clung to the vain hope that something would happen if only they waited patiently.

The floor of the mow will probably soon break under the crushing weight on it. – A still, heavy stream drifted down through the darkness from above and entered into each man who had come. Each of them had a room prepared to receive the stream.

When the room is full, I'll sink.

They started up and looked around.

We're waiting.

We have nothing to wait for.

We're still waiting.

At one time this evening wild rumors and half truths had spread among them. Now that was over. They no longer invented such things and let them grow and sent them on. They just waited.

If they looked out the windows they saw something strange. From the barn, with all its stalls and pens and burdens, the shining light up at the house took the form of a sight joyous almost beyond belief. An incomprehensible light streamed out from two windows, from the depths of a joyous, luminous ship sailing through the night.

Look at the ship!

They could see it by just turning their heads a bit. It was not for them. We're *here*, our hands and feet fettered. We're not sailing through the night.

Someone stepped close to Karl Lee. He was standing near the door so that anyone who entered the barn met him first. It was his wife who had come.

She touched his arm.

It was a large part of his world that had come; his busy, varied everyday world. And also his quiet rest and comfort.

She said softly:

'Is Rolf here with you?'

'No, he's off somewhere else.'

He heard the thankfulness in her voice because Rolf still lived.

'He hasn't left again, I'm sure of that,' he said. 'What do you want him for?'

'Nothing.'

They listened to the humming silence around them. What did Mari Lee want? She must have known that Rolf had not left again. There was something else on her mind.

'Did you just come down, Mari?' he asked.

'Yes, I had to.'

She said it as if a resistance had been broken, and she had been compelled to come.

He looked up at the house, to see if the light had been extinguished. No, it was still there. Inga's room sailed along as before, but Mari Lee had left it. It was not for her, either.

He thought he understood her, but asked just the same:

'Wouldn't you rather go back up to the house? There's nothing to stay down here for.'

She did not answer, nor did he expect an answer.

Her nearness was comforting. He could have thanked her because she no longer shut herself off from him up in the house. She also finally had to find her way to the barn. He could not see her face clearly. He knew every detail of it, but at that moment he longed to see it once again.

I had to, she had said. She did not go home.

No one went home. They were all so despairing, each for his own reason, that they could not flee, or explain it away. All these reduced and horrified people had been drawn to the barn by their victim lying there. Now Mari Lee had also been drawn in. There seemed to be a silent agreement among them to hold vigil there that night.

'What have you said to them, Karl?'

He answered bitterly, feebly:

'Nothing. I couldn't say to them either what I should have or what I wanted to.'

She walked away. So they too could both be alone with their thoughts. Rolf was somewhere else. Where are you to whom I can open my heart, and who can burn it pure? They listened for Kari Ness. She was not there. She was now only a voice that had grown silent. The night was dark, and the silence grew deeper and deeper. From somewhere came the sound of animals once more sleeping in boundless innocence.

20

EACH MAN BY HIMSELF. All who had come to the barn. Although they were closely bound together by that which had drawn them there, each one of them had his own problems that no one else needed to see – and which he alone could solve.

Impatient waiting from the first. Waiting for something to break in and help them. One long hour after the other passed in vain. The night just moved along silently in its wonted course. Those who lay at the bottom of the pit would just have to lie there. Those who were so made that nothing bothered them had already left.

The long night of waiting made them sensitive to all within them – and one secret cache after another opened up and showed its contents. Such am I; let me do penance.

Each of them wished for a white flame into which he could throw all his evil deeds, but knew that he would have to carry them with him. The night moved slowly through the barn and bent them further down. Such am I; the pit is in my brow, but I have tried to rid myself of it.

They all knew that there were people in the pig pens. In their own despair they saw them there in the dust, and opened still another secret cache while no one was looking.

Now there's nothing more left that I know of –

The weight on the floor of the mow pressed down on them. No one knew what Hill and Dale were doing now. They had withdrawn, nameless, back among the others and no longer thought about gaining absolution at their expense. The storm rushing through the barn swept all such thoughts before it. It was not now a question of struggling upward, but of gazing into the depths within oneself.

Where was Rolf? Where was Else? Gudrun, Ivar, Jens, all of them. No one called to them, they could stay where they were, helpless in their bonds. The night was long, they had ample time to discover what they really were.

But the night passed. The hours edged onward, minute by tiny minute that each struck sharply at their nerves. They imagined that the barn shook, so deeply sunk in despair as they were. Now they thought they understood everything, and took everything upon themselves.

Their lanterns vanished one by one. Some burned out and smoked themselves dead, others were blown out in secret. Those on the right and left need not see what they did and how they looked.

And thus the barn also vanished. It was the lanterns that had made it visible. Now it sank into the night and became one with everything else that was pitch dark. There was no light other than that up at the house, sailing through the night as before. Solitary, free and wondrous.

Rolf started up at the sound of heavy tramping on the wooden floor. It was impossible to say what time it was. He was completely exhausted by his futile struggling and was seized by fear at the unexpected thumping. Then he saw a faint light filtering through the windows and into the barn. Day was about to break. He got a grip on himself and heard that it was something large and heavy walking about and tramping on the floor with hard shoes. It was the horse. Now he could see the outline of the animal in the growing half-light. Soon after he felt Black Lady's breath against his face and a firm, friendly nose nudged at him, accompanied by the fragrance of green hay and oats.

Jens must have let Black Lady out, as a sort of conclusion to his period of penance in the stable. He had found help for himself, and therefore let the mare out to the others.

Jens himself was not to be seen. But Black Lady came tramping through the barn and brought with her memories of innumerable days filled with work and the squeaking of wagon wheels and the smell of the sun on old harness. It was strange, but the smell of Black Lady reminded them first and foremost of the sun. It came as a greeting from God and an exhortation once more to take heart and carry on. Because everything around them carried on. Look, there goes Black Lady!

She had never before been allowed to wander freely in the barn, so she took great joy in it. Waded in the hay, tramped on the floor, amusing herself by poking into every corner – and everywhere there were people who started and woke up and blessed her.

The rooster began to crow, and they heard that it was morning. That did its share to raise their spirits and give them courage.

They found that they could think differently again. Karl Lee's huge barn was to store produce in. Hay and grain poured through its doors, and outside the sun poured down day after day and gave life and strength – and perhaps also happiness, though that still seemed somehow beyond belief.

They felt that it said:

Rise up from your fall.

Rolf heard it too. Rise up from your fall, Rolf. This is not the end. He stood up, weary and doubting.

Black Lady clomped through the barn.

Strengthened by this, Gudrun suddenly spoke out and broke the long silence. The horse's wandering about, and the raising of heads that it caused supplied her with courage and need. Before they knew it she had stepped forth into the half-light by a window and said clearly, and defiantly because it was not easy to say it before all her neighbors:

'I'm going to have a baby, you know – !'

She said no more. But it fitted in with what they were thinking themselves. She had spoken for them, too. They were thankful to her. Listen – Gudrun has stood up among the ruins, and is with child. We're not crushed and cursed.

The floor of the mow creaked. Hill and Dale were alive and moving around. Black Lady was still wandering about, inquisitive and pleased. Every sound was good. Only the door leading to the pig pens was still tightly closed. No sound came from there.

It grew lighter. They saw Karl Lee catch Black Lady and lead her away. The barn had come forth out of the night and was once again a building with sharp outlines.

Karl Lee found Jens in the stable when he put Black Lady in. Jens was awake and quiet, everything within him burned pure for a while.

'Here's Black Lady.'

'Yes, she got out,' Jens replied.

Karl Lee left. The growing half-light streamed in grey rays through every opening, and they once more could see. People stood up wearily and stretched their legs. Some brushed hay and straw off their clothes. No one wished to speak to anyone else yet, but they felt a strong common bond. They had settled their accounts with themselves and found strength for a new wearisome wandering through life.

Karl Lee walked past and opened the door to the pig pens. He was met by small grunts and squeals, and several abject people rose, grey as the dawn, out of the dust into which they had bowed themselves. And Kari Ness was there! It startled him to see that. She fled before he could get a good look at her. The others stood and blinked. Karl Lee hardly dared speak to them.

'It's morning,' he said.

He could just barely make out the form of the boar behind the planks of his pen, his tusks protruding from his jaws, his pitted brow dark and narrow.

It's morning, Karl Lee had said. It sounded in reality as if he had said: come out now! and they obeyed blindly. They had kept vigil and bled bitterly. They passed through the barn, and noticed that it now was easier to breathe there. They walked almost shamefully out of the building. They kept their eyes on the ground and did not look at each other.

It became so light that all the people were driven out of the barn which no longer contained what they needed. It stood there towering above them, used up and extinguished. They came out one after the other. Mari Lee came out. She went over to her husband as soon as she saw him. They saw Rolf come out too.

No one felt like speaking. They walked in silence across the barn-yard. It was not raining and had become cooler. The sea was grey. Hill and Dale came down out of the mow and disappeared among the others. A morning breeze stroked them gently. They shivered, fragile as leaves. They had suffered much – but had risen to their feet again.

A woman's voice said, to them all:

'Look: the island is as green as ever!'

It was Gudrun again, she who was carrying a tiny life within her. She needed to affirm that life would continue.

Yes, they saw it, all of them, and paused while it took hold of them and brought things forth in them. It was so light now that they could see clearly. The island was green. Karl Lee's orchard was just as fertile and generous as ever. It was only they who had been cast to the ground.

But they had been able to rise up again. There must have been a seed in the dust that had grown to strength and hope within them. Their eyes cleared, they saw how steady in its course runs that which calls forth life and death. The sun would soon return, and the grass and leaves were green. It was God's greeting to the frightened and tormented.

They stood and shivered in the breeze, and saw what they had to do: return to their accustomed places, and remember what they had settled within themselves that night. The island is ours, and it is green.

They walked away, each with his own concerns. Gudrun walked least weighed down of all. Hill and Dale tried to swing their huge workmen's hands a tiny bit at their sides. The people from the pig pens walked along with downcast eyes, as if their shame were still with them. Kari Ness had fled. But they knew she would soon reappear. Jens stood over by the old well where the sows had been killed. Bergit was already on the way to the tiny motherless pigs with warm milk. Rolf stood without moving as Else walked past. They looked at each other. A last farewell.

Then Rolf turned toward the sea, to look for a boat, the boat that would take him away. He knew it would not come as early as this, but was nevertheless already watching for it. It would come as surely as the sun would soon rise. It could not be hindered. He had tried to resign himself to its coming.

The bewitching light up at the house had lost its power now that day had come. All that was left of it were two pale windows high up on the wall. There was nothing about them reminiscent of a journey now.

His mother said:

'Is it here you are, Rolf.'

He saw his father and mother standing beside him, as quiet as all the others. But he saw thanks in the sleepless eyes they turned toward him. They clearly told him that it was right that he was alive. There had been death enough.

He was able to believe that, too, as hopeless as everything looked. His father asked:

'Are you looking for the boat ?'

'Yes.'

'Well, you still have time to come into the house with us for a while.'

Also by
TARJEI VESAAS
and published by Peter Owen

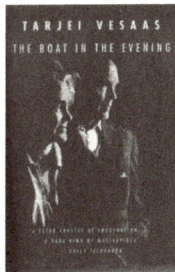

The Boat in the Evening
A crane colony arrives at its breeding ground to play out a
delicate drama that ends with the ceremony of the ritual dance.
All is observed by a transfixed child who has frozen into his
background and become a piece of nature himself. Unfolding in
a series of sketches that record the changing moods of human
experience, *The Boat in the Evening* is at once pervaded by a sense
of melancholy and a sensuous appreciation of nature.
Peter Owen Modern Classic / 978-0-7206-1198-4 / £9.95
'A book of great strength and beauty' – *The Times*
'A rare mixture of creative vitality, conviction and artistry' – *Guardian*

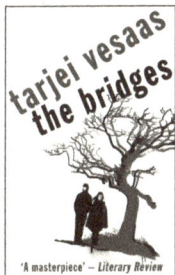

TARJEI VESAAS The Bridges
The Bridges describes the changing relationship between three
adolescents – an unmarried mother who has drowned her newborn
child and the girl and boy who befriend her. Their individual reactions
to the tragedy and their efforts to communicate with each other form
the central theme of the narrative. As strange, unsettling and as
memorable as Vesaas's masterpieces *The Ice Palace* and *The Birds*, this
remarkable work of fiction conveys the compassion, insight and lyrical
power of a great Scandinavian novel.
Peter Owen Modern Classic / 978-0-7206-1639-5 / £9.99
'Brilliant concentration of style and feeling . . . Vesaas is clearly an
important writer.' – *The Times*

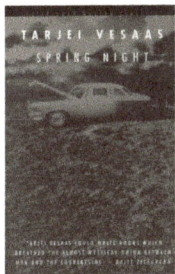

Spring Night
Teenager Sissel and her young brother Olaf have been left minding
their parents' farm for the night. But when a strange family descends
on them, lost, in a broken-down car, the children have to cope alone,
and by the end of the spring night there has been not only a birth but
a death in the house, and adolescence has vanished for ever. *Spring
Night* is a beautifully observed portrait of the death of innocence.
Peter Owen Modern Classic / 978-0-7206-1189-2 / £9.95
'Tarjei Vesaas could write books which breathed the almost
mystical union between man and countryside.' – *Daily Telegraph*
'Vesaas achieves his effects with a powerful economy of words.'
– *Guardian*

THE ICE PALACE
Tarjei Vesaas
978-0-7206-2014-6 • 176pp • £12.99

Peter Owen Cased Classic

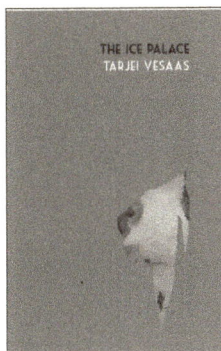

'How simple this novel is. How subtle. How strong. How unlike any other. It is unique. It is unforgettable. It is extraordinary.' – Doris Lessing, *Independent*

'It is hard to do justice to *The Ice Palace* . . . The narrative is urgent, the descriptions relentlessly beautiful, the meaning as powerful as the ice piling up on the lake.' – *The Times*

'Vesaas's laconic sentences are as cold and simple as ice – and as fantastic.' – *Telegraph*

Siss and Unn are new friends – so new that they have spent only one whole evening in each other's company. But so profound is that evening that when Unn inexplicably disappears Siss's world is shattered. Siss's struggle with her fidelity to the memory of her friend and Unn's fatal exploration of the strange, terrifyingly beautiful frozen waterfall that is the Ice Palace are described in prose of a lyrical economy that ranks among the most memorable achievements of modern literature.

Tarjei Vesaas is regarded as one of the finest writers ever to have come out of Scandinavia – he is notable for having been nominated for the Nobel Prize three times and has been considered one of the greatest prose stylists never to have won. Nevertheless, his reputation is secure and growing all the time. Peter Owen has long considered *The Ice Palace* to be the greatest work ever to have come from his publishing house, which boasts seven Nobel Prize winners on its list.

Peter Owen Publishers

www.peterowen.com

E: info@peterowen.com

@PeterOwenPubs

Facebook: Peter Owen Publishers

Independent publishers since 1951